SHOWDOWN!

Ord went for his gun. He was fast. He was practiced in his trade. He was good, and he knew it, and he went for his right-hand gun. His hand dropped with the speed of a striking rattlesnake, a blur of action, and the heavy pistol was halfway out of its holster when the blur stopped suddenly. The owner of that very fast hand was looking into the deadly muzzle of Slocum's .31.

"Don't try it," said Slocum bitterly. "I'd just as soon blow your brains out as look at you."

OTHER BOOKS BY JAKE LOGAN

JAKE LOGAN

RAWHIDE JUSTICE

BERKLEY BOOKS, NEW YORK

RAWHIDE JUSTICE

A Berkley Book/published by arrangement with
the author

PRINTING HISTORY
Berkley edition/November 1986

ISBN: 0-425-09342-5

A BERKLEY BOOK ® TM 757,375
Berkley Books are published by The Berkley Publishing Group,
200 Madison Avenue, New York, NY 10016.
The name "BERKLEY" and the stylized "B" with design are trademarks
belonging to Berkley Publishing Corporation.

PRINTED IN THE UNITED STATES OF AMERICA

1

It was a hard sun, but John Slocum's already taut nerves stiffened under a chill. He had brought five thousand head of longhorns a thousand miles. It had been a grueling journey north through Texas, Indian Territory, and now into Kansas. Storms had sandblasted his herd and his men, Indians had demanded tolls, petty rustlers had badgered them. The land itself, a monotonous world of flat plains and low rolling hills, gave no relief. Instead, the land hindered progress with swift-water rivers that snatched a hundred longhorn lives. There were areas of inadequate grass, where the herd went hungry, and there was dust.

Dust. There had been a thousand miles of dust. There wasn't a man in Slocum's crew who had seen his face clearly while shaving during the last few months. Companion to dust was sweat. Sweat stained the bands of sombreros, caked shirts and the crotches of trousers with salty grime. Sweat cracked lips and peeled noses and forced the eyes to narrow down, so that a man looked like a lobo wolf on the hunt.

Just a few more days pushing the herd and they would reach their destination, Dodge City. There were hot baths in Dodge, and the grime would slide away in soapy water. There was drink in Dodge, good stiff bar whiskey, food that would stick to a man's innards and not be full of sand and grit, whatever a man could afford. And there were women. Slocum allowed himself a smile. God, how he would welcome a woman again, any woman. Long months of abstinence had brought him to such a peak that he didn't care who the woman might be. She could teach Sunday school or follow the trade of the soiled dove at the Longhorn Saloon. It didn't matter to Slocum, as long as the woman was willing.

Just a few more days and the drive would be over. Why did he feel so edgy, then? He would soon unload his responsibilities, collect twenty-five thousand dollars for the herd, and be a free man. What was it about this early evening that tauted his nerves and caused him to sit ramrod-straight in the saddle?

His green eyes slid to the sun again. It was a hard yellow orb, burning bright, though it fanned the surrounding skies with beautiful shades of red. It was a beautiful sunset, yet troubling, as if blood streaked the horizon.

Suddenly Slocum understood. There had been just such a sun in the sky at Gettysburg. As sergeant in charge of a platoon of sharpshooters, it had been his duty to pick off Union officers. Using a Spencer repeating rifle ripped from the pale fingers of a dead Union infantryman, he had killed all day. With passionless accuracy he had bloodied the blue tunics of Union officers. It was not his way to wound, but to kill. A wounded man could heal, return to the battlefields, and slay Confederates.

The sun had been hard during the killing, burning his mind free of remorse, and he had slaughtered many. It was a job he had been assigned. He hadn't liked the job, but it was his, and he performed well.

Not until after the War, when he stood on the dilapidated acreage of the family farm in Georgia, did the awfulness of what had occurred hit him. He had killed Yankees before that day, but not so often, and not without some regret. That day he had become a killer, but as he surveyed the ruins of the farm, the ghosts of a recent past marched before his eyes. None of those he had shot were much older than he, and many were younger: Boys, children hardly dry behind the ears, had stood up to deadly Confederate fire. They had been brave, but they had perished. Families grieved for their lost ones, and wives wept in the secret night for long months as the War growled to a close.

John Slocum had found the reason for his uneasiness. The sun, yellow and streaked with blood, reminded him of a time he would rather forget and the remembering served as a catharsis. The chill melted from his spine, but Slocum took the negative emotion as a bad sign. Trouble was brewing. It might be for him or for somebody he knew, but trouble was on the way.

The sun released its hold on the earth and sank out of sight. As the world darkened, Slocum called out, "Hey, Ned, come here!"

A young cowboy nudged his horse over. He was a lean man, thin as the foreleg of the pinto he rode. His eyes were narrowed, and they seemed more wolfish than those of his companions.

"You ride night herd," Slocum instructed him. "I smell trouble tonight. That red sky we had at dawn could mean a storm over the horizon. The cattle are right spooky. Some kind of trouble is coming tonight."

The cowboy's slitted eyes froze.

"Trouble, boss? You sure? Looks like a calm sky to me."

"You never heard those old sailors' chanties? 'Red sky

at night, sailor's delight. Red sky at morning, sailor take warning.'"

"Yeah, I heard 'em. But it don't feel like no storm. The cattle are jumpy, though."

"Yeah. Well, you take the first shift, and Bobby will relieve you at midnight."

Ned Blake's eyes lost their frost. He half grinned, tossed his hand in salute, and rejoined the herd.

Slocum watched Ned as he disappeared into the dusty twilight. Ned was difficult to figure out. He played his hand close, never said much, kept to himself a lot. Still, he was a good hand, and gave no cause for suspicion. In spite of that, Slocum wouldn't have kept him on, but Ned was the brother of Earl Blake, a partner in the present enterprise. You didn't fire your partner's brother just because you didn't like him. If the young cowboy's slitted eyes seemed to be watching all the time, taking in every move that Slocum, the other men, and the cattle made, there was likely nothing more to it than youthful curiosity, or maybe the fellow was looking after his brother's interests. Slocum admitted his imagination was probably working overtime, and yet he had lived with danger often enough to sense its presence. Ned Blake was, in some way, a threat.

The herd came to a halt near the chuck wagon. Cooky, a short man with an upturned Prussian moustache, had the evening meal ready. Only Slocum knew that the man's real name was Pluto G. Manstead, a name that somehow seemed to belong to a scholar, not a cook on a long trail drive. The men knew him only as Cooky, which was enough, as far as they were concerned, and he was one of the best pot burners in the West. Slocum had actually bid for him at quiet, man-to-man meetings, because so many outfits were after his skills. Slocum had won in the bidding with one hundred dollars a month, plus a bonus if the man stuck for the entire trip. A good cook was worth his weight in gold. All the men had to look forward to were meals. If the food was satisfactory—plenty of pastry and hot biscuits, good steaks and beans and flapjacks—there was content in the ranks. Poor cooks could cause entire crews to walk off, and trail bosses would hock their souls to Beelzebub for a good one.

As the cattle settled, the men turned their horses over to the wrangler and joined the line at the chuck wagon. They jerked their bedrolls from the wagon's box and spread them on the grounnd. They consumed their food silently, for they were too weary for talk. Sunup till sundown was a long day. After the meal, they rolled cigarettes and relaxed on their blankets, and small talk began.

"I hear we only got fifty mile er so t' Dodge."

"Two, three more days."

"An' then I can get these goddamned lice off me in a tub of boilin' water!"

"Hell, it'd take a tub of boilin' axle grease to kill what you got, Curley."

A snicker passed among the men. Curley, so called because of a thick mat of tangled blond hair, snorted.

"I ain't got what none of you fellers ain't got." He scratched. "Hot damn!"

"Anybody's got a bath on his mind first, probably got the holes in his front pockets wide open," came another observation.

More snickers.

"Wouldn't matter where you're concerned, Bobby."

"How many times in Fort Worth, Bobby?"

Bobby wasn't a man in years. He was eighteen, dark-haired, dark-eyed, white of tooth, and coming into the prime of his lust.

"Hell," said Bobby proudly, "six times in one night, but you gotta remember, I was preparin' for a long time without."

"Me," came a soft voice in back of a cigarette's red glow, "I'm goin' t' get a good feed."

"Tubby, you could eat your way through the China Wall, stones and all of it."

"Damn right," agreed Tubby, who lived up to his name with more loose flesh than his mounts wanted to carry. "Cooky's good, here, but I got a yen for some Chinese stuff."

"You gotta have dollars, not yens," scoffed another voice. "Besides, there ain't no Chinese joints in Dodge."

"So if there ain't, I'll make it myself," said Tubby.

"Hell, you couldn't cook a boot."

Slocum listened to the talk without joining in. Since coming to the West from his home state of Georgia thirteen years before, he had heard many similar discussions. When the men drew near civilization after a long absence, dreams flew in the air like sparks from the fire. If Tubby wanted Chinese food, likely he would get something close to it, anyway. On the trail, a man lived on his dreams, and it was a matter of great personal satisfaction to come away with at least a part of them. Most guys opted for a bath, a woman, a quart of bad whiskey or good whiskey, if he could afford it. Those were practical dreams that could be realized. Tubby wasn't being practical, and he was being subjected to some good-natured ragging.

Slocum turned to the man next to him. "Ken, you better ride with Blake tonight."

The figure grunted. "Can't he handle it alone?"

"Yes."

"What then?" The voice took on a shade of interest.

Slocum lowered his voice. "I don't know about him. His eyes have been pinched all day, like a panther cat ready to kill."

"He's an odd one."

"He's more than odd. I don't trust him, even if he is my partner's brother. You go out and cover the west flank in an hour. If Blake asks, tell him I smell a storm. Tell him anything you want, but just be there."

"Good enough."

"I'll send Tubby and Bobby to relieve you at midnight."

"Right."

Slocum glanced sideways at the man, pleased. He never got any arguments from Ken Dorsey. Ken had been his assistant on the drive, and Slocum couldn't have found a better man in Texas, though Dorsey was actually a Kansan. He had hired Dorsey as a regular hand, but before they'd gone a hundred miles he knew he had a man expert in the business. Dorsey had been on several trail drives, and his experience showed.

Blake had been Slocum's original assistant. As the brother of the man who was supplying money for this enterprise, it would be expected that he would have authority. But Blake didn't know his hands from his hat about handling cattle, and that had showed up quickly, too.

Blake hadn't liked being replaced, but had to admit his ignorance, and had stepped down. He soon seemed to forget his pique, and was smoothly pleasant to both Slocum and Dorsey. Slocum didn't like that. He knew Earl Blake too well not to believe that some of the man's oily characteristics hadn't rubbed off on his younger brother. Slocum didn't like Earl either, but work was work, and he didn't see where he could go wrong on a straightforward deal. He was to bring the cows to Dodge for a percentage of the sale, and a salary to boot. Slocum had everything to gain and nothing to lose. It was sweet, except that lately he'd had the feeling that all was not well. He couldn't put a finger on the reason—Ned Blake's phony cheerfulness, or a growing doubt about Earl—something. All he knew was that the closer they got to Dodge, the more uneasy he became.

Dorsey left and Slocum settled down. Before he slid out of his boots he called to the relief guard.

"Bobby, you and Tubs relieve the watch at midnight."

The two groaned. Both were youngsters, for whom sleep was a goddess. To leave a warm nest of blankets at midnight was not a welcome future, but neither argued.

There was discipline on a trail drive. There had to be. Without discipline, without one man in total charge, like the captain of a ship, anarchy would result, even rebellion. Slocum had known of trail bosses who lost entire crews because they lost control of the men.

The two cowboys groaned and moaned, but they rolled up in their blankets and were fast asleep before the last moan softened in the night air.

Slocum grinned. Kids! Many in his crew of ten were under twenty-two or twenty-three years of age. Trail driving was romantic, and it beckoned many youngsters from both the West and the East. After a few trips, the drives became a way of life. It became what a man knew, and he did it because it was his work. It put beans on the table, but the romance wore off, leaving the dust and sweat and stink and dangers to cope with. The older men were a cynical bunch, but steady and dependable. A man's reputation was his meal ticket, and an experienced trail hand was in demand. For thirty a month they found they never got rich, but Rusty, one of the older men, pointed out, "I'll have me a hell of a time in Dodge. Two hundred in my pockets one day, two cents the next; what's so bad about that?"

A married man might have been more conservative, but for the single men that was the pattern of life. Work hard, play hard, until they died of accident, disease, a bullet, or of old age at forty-five.

As Slocum lay under a blanket, his thoughts drifted to women. Bobby wasn't the only wild cock in the crew. In his mind, he pictured women of the past. He saw their naked bodies, the pink nipples, the moist inner thighs, and his penis stiffened. He was too mature for the "hole in the pocket" routine, but damn, how he wanted a woman.

He closed his mind off to his self-torture with a deliberate effort. There was little use in fanning the flames. He would be in Dodge soon enough, and change fantasy to reality.

He was deep asleep, beyond dreaming, when he was awakened by loud noises. There were shouts and pistol shots, and the thunder of many hooves.

Slocum leaped up, slipped into his boots, and strapped on his gunbelt in the same swift motion. Others were also struggling out of sleep and into the harsh awakening.

The cattle were on the move, and Slocum knew at once that rustlers were at work. There were more shouts from the darkness, and shots sent flashes into the night. His own night watch would have no reason for firing guns.

"You men get to the front of the herd and try to stop it!" he cried above the racket.

"Ken!" He called. "Ken!"

No response. Slocum glanced at the sky, and by the dim starlight, seeing how the stars had shifted position, reckoned the time at a shade past midnight. Bobby and Tubby would just be changing places with Dorsey and Blake.

Slocum's green eyes pierced the gloom, trying to make out who was where and doing what. He saw a dozen dark shapes forcing the cattle into action. The shapes were not his men. He knew the silhouettes of his crew. The way they rode was engraved on his mind after a thousand miles. The shapes were rustlers.

Slocum drew his pistol, a percussion Navy Colt .31. He aimed at a shadow and squeezed the trigger. The shape reeled in its saddle but kept going. Slocum raced to the head of the herd, and along with his men, fired into the ground at the feet of the panicking herd.

When the Colt was empty, he slammed it home in its holster and drew another. This was in a holster which had been covered by a flap to keep the caps and powder dry. Slocum wore his weapons with the handles facing forward. He felt this was the best method for a fast cross-draw—a theory that experience had proved correct—but right now he was cursing.

The flap of the spare pistol was held down with a thong,

and he couldn't unhook it. His horse, a spotted critter from the remudas of Nez Percé Indians east of the Rockies, was twisting and turning in fear. The charging cattle, their long horns flashing in the dim light, would have caused a fence post to duck, and Wind, the horse, was much more lively than a post.

"Damn it all," yelled Slocum, "hold still, will you? So's I can get this damned flap free."

Wind heard his master, but with cloven-hoofed flesh weighing as much and more as he beared down by the hundreds, it wasn't easy. He tossed and bucked, while long, thick horns thrust at his sides like the thin, deadly sabres of Spanish Conquistadors.

Slocum finally unleashed his spare pistol, but he didn't fire it into the ground. The cattle were in full run now, and pistol shots were not going to stop them. He saved his lead for the rustlers.

Then he noticed something. The dust had thickened to the consistency of marsh fog. Even so, he should have been able to spot Ned Blake. It was difficult to see the others, who by now had escaped to either side of the rampaging herd, but he did see them. Not so Blake. The premonition that Slocum had experienced earlier returned. Was Blake in on this? He squinted against the dust and realized he couldn't make out the familiar shapes of Dorsey, Bobby, or Tubs either. Premonitions carried their own spirit, reached their own dreadful conclusions. What sort of climax did this one have in store?

Slocum urged Wind toward the far side of the herd in an effort to join his men. In the meantime, more shouts and cries sounded, and the cattle bawled with excitement. Intent on locating his crew, Slocum didn't see the charging steer that slammed into Wind. Wind staggered, and Slocum was catapulted from the saddle. His head crashed against a boulder, and he dove into darkness.

When he opened his eyes again, Wind was grazing calmly nearby. There was a long but shallow gash on his flank. He looked at Slocum, who sat up groggily.

"You poor bastard," muttered Slocum, "you nearly got it, didn't you?"

Wind whickered gently and returned to grazing. The problems of men were not for him. Getting enough grass was, and he had found a patch.

"For that matter," said his master, "so did I."

It was a fortunate chance that Slocum had reached the far side of the herd, or he would have been trampled. Wind had been charged by a panicked stray. Slocum climbed painfully to his feet. The world swirled for a moment, then settled reluctantly. It was dawn now, and all he could see was the empty plain. The rustlers had made a clean getaway.

The chuck wagon, half a mile back, hunkered on the prairie, dark and somehow ominous, like a brand-new tombstone. Again a premonition invaded Slocum's objecting mind. He rode slowly toward the wagon, not wanting to see what he knew he was going to see.

Cooky and several men were ringed around three figures lying at strange ease on the ground. Slocum dismounted and walked over slowly.

"We was comin' for you next, boss," Cooky began.

Slocum waved him to silence.

He stared at the three figures, and his premonition burst upon him like hellfire. Bobby, Tubby, and Ken Dorsey lay dead. Dorsey had been shot—blood spread over the front of his shirt attested to that—but both Bobby and his friend had been trampled to death.

"God," muttered Slocum. "Great God."

He had seen men blown to pieces by cannon fire at Bull Run; he had seen men with their guts hanging through their fingers after a bayonet charge. A comrade's horse had been killed by a Union sniper, and the horse fell over, crushing his friend so badly that his eyes popped from their sockets. But Slocum had never seen a man trampled by a thousand hooves.

The two young men were battered beyond recognition, their faces crushed to a pulp, their limbs broken and shattered, bones sticking through their clothing—their clothing being the only thing recognizable about the two.

"God," repeated Slocum.

"We was coming after you next," Cooky repeated, "but we thought you had been trampled . . ."

Slocum understood. Two mangled bodies were more than a man could stand, but three? He nodded grimly.

Poor Bobby. He would never get that girl now. No more six times in one night. Tubby would not taste the object of his dreams, Chinese food.

As for Ken—well, Ken hadn't asked for much at all. Not women or Chinese food or anything. He was saving his money, sending it to his sister, because one day he wanted his own ranch. That was Ken—practical. He was going to do something with his life. . . . *Was*.

Damn it!

Slocum looked around. The rest of the crew were all right, though in shock from what they were seeing.

"Where's Ned Blake?" he asked Cooky. "Did he show up?"

"I think," ventured a cowhand known as Blondy, because of his hair. "I think . . ." He paused.

"What?" barked Slocum.

"Well, I think he went with them rustlers," finished Blondy.

A couple of the others nodded.

"Yeah, I seen that," said Curley.

"An' it looked to me," said yet another, "like he was shooting at Dorsey here. I think Dorsey was on to him."

"Did Dorsey shoot back?"

The cowboy shrugged. "Hell, boss, they was so much dust and noise and cattle all over the place, I didn't see all that much, but yeah, I think he squeezed off one or two rounds."

Slocum knelt by the body of his friend, his *segundo* for three months.

"If you didn't get him," he said gently, "by God, *I* swear I will."

He stood up, and said crisply, "All right, we got some burying to do. And then—" His voice hardened—"we got some people to find."

2

As Slocum stood by the body of Dorsey, the old feeling returned, a feeling he had known before. It boiled up in him unbidden, a human weakness that he could not control under the circumstances. Revenge. Slocum's green eyes turned flinty and cold as his pity and fury mounted. Somebody, for no good reason, had killed three of his men. One had been shot—by whom? Some nameless renegade of the night? A brute with a lust for killing? Or could it have been Ned Blake? Blake, the sly one, Blake the odd-card, easy-going type, Blake, the brother of Earl, partner in this project. If so, why? Why would brother turn against brother? Slocum had seen that in the War between the States, but those were ideological differences. This was business. Ned stood to gain by delivering the cattle safely, for there would be other drives, bigger cuts of the profits.

Did Ned Blake have a connection with this? Slocum suspected he did. The man should have fired warning shots at the first sign of trouble, but, as far as Slocum knew, Blake had not.

"You men hear anything before the cattle started running?"

There were negative replies.

"All's I heard was them hooves poundin'," stated Blondy.

The others agreed.

Their testimony helped substantiate Slocum's suspicions. A nightrider was supposed to call the alarm in case of trouble. If he expected a storm was brewing that might spook the herd, he asked for another rider or two. If the cattle were restless for no reason known to man, the nightrider asked for more men, because a collective restlessness could lead to a stampede. It was the same as a mob of humans. Slocum had seen lynchings because of a mob, the mob acting together. Individually, the men involved would have shuddered at the thought of killing another man by strangling him with a rope, but in a mob, each one became a different man. So it was with cattle.

"What we going t' do about this?" asked Curley. He was close to tears, for he and Bobby had been of an age, and friends.

"Anybody see which direction the herd went?"

Slocum was recovering from the blow to his head, and the sight of his dead.

"They lit out toward Dodge," said another cowboy, a deeply tanned, middle-aged man called Rusty.

"You stay here," Slocum said to Cooky, "and maybe start digging a grave for them." He indicated the dead. "We have to do some looking."

He realized that his force of men was small, perhaps too small to do any good. Yet one never knew. During the War, he had single-handedly captured a dozen Yankees, when he caught them sleeping. You never knew. Out of ten men, three were dead, and Cooky was digging their grave. That left six besides himself. The six were good men. Some of them were young, perhaps inexperienced in the ways of exchanging lead with another man, but they were angry and grieving, and the two emotions would carry them into a fight easily.

They rode toward Dodge at a trot. The horses were fresh, in spite of the night's excitement. Slocum could feel the power in Wind's muscles as he moved smoothly over the slightly rolling countryside. He liked spotted horses, and he had one under him whenever possible. They were strong, long on stamina, and sure-footed. They were also loyal. Wind had waited for him that morning. He hadn't panicked and run off across the prairie. He had found a bunch of grass, and grazed while waiting for the man who was his boss to give another order.

Slocum leaned forward and patted Wind's neck.

"Good boy," he murmured, and the horse's ears flicked back, then forward.

The trail of the herd was easy to follow. Five thousand longhorns, minus a couple of hundred in losses and tribute to Indians, left a trail an Eastern stockbroker could track.

Slocum looked at the eastern horizon, figured the time by the sun's position. He put it a shade past six. The rustlers had a six-hour lead, and by the sign, the cattle were being moved swiftly. It didn't matter to the rustlers if a few were lost to accident or exhaustion. They would still have plenty of free cows when they reached their destination. It was all profit—except, and Slocum allowed a grim smile, for the man he had shot. Maybe Ken had got a man, too, before he was murdered.

He was in the lead when they topped a rise and found Ned Blake.

Blake's horse grazed nearby, even as Wind had done when Slocum was toppled. The horse was busily chomping grass, and when Slocum mounted the rise, the horse looked up and whickered.

But Ned Blake didn't move. He lay very still, flat on his back. Blood covered the front of his shirt, just as it had

Ken Dorsey's. The man's eyes were open and staring at the sky. The sun burned into them, casting bright rays back, a glitter as though they still possessed life, but they would never blink again. Slocum cursed under his breath and a muscle quivered in his cheek. He turned away from the dead man, his throat constricting suddenly as if his rage would choke him.

Slocum and the others dismounted. They stood around the body, speaking in low tones.

"Whaddya suppose happened?"

"Well, somebody gave him a good one, that's fer sure."

"I wonder if the bastard was in with them rustlers."

"We gonna bury him?"

A brief thought passed through Slocum's mind. Dorsey had been seen firing his pistol. Could it have been he who killed Blake?

Slocum knelt beside the body. He unbuttoned the shirt gently. A dead man deserved a certain amount of respect, no matter who he was. Many shots had been fired. Slocum had himself hit one of the rustlers. Could it have been his own ball that was fatal to Blake? Slocum wanted to know.

The wound was large. Dorsey carried a Colt Walker .44, while Slocum's pistol was a .31 caliber. He checked the exit wound. A bullet will flatten, enlarge to another caliber when it hits tissue, muscle, or bone. The wound where the ball came out was big, larger than .44 caliber. Slocum hadn't killed Ned. Chances were it had been Dorsey who fired the fatal shot.

Slocum stood up.

"His lamp out?" asked Blondy.

"Yeah, permanent," he said. "We'll bury him."

Blake's pistol and gunbelt were taken, and the few personal belongings in his pocket. Nobody had thought to bring a shovel or a pick, so it was not possible to dig a grave. Rocks and big boulders had to serve, and they were heaped over the body until it was completely covered.

"Least that'll keep the coyotes from him," muttered Rusty.

Slocum nodded and pointed at the trail.

"Let's go," he said. "We got to see where the cattle are."

"That all you give a damn about, Slocum? Your god-damned cattle?" Rusty was close to the edge. Maybe the killing had unnerved him, set something off inside him.

"The ones who have the cattle are the ones who murdered some good men," Slocum said tightly. Rusty swallowed and turned away.

The men put spurs to their horses again, and got them moving, as if relieved to get away from the scene of death. Ned Blake had not been liked, but as one of the younger men said, "Jesus, he looked so final."

And there would be more of the same when they returned to the chuck wagon, where Cooky was digging a place for their friends. Altogether, it was more than a depressing situation, and the younger men hung back some.

Slocum sensed their feelings, but he was determined to find his herd. He pressed on, his green eyes steely once more. His lips were a thin line, a crease in his weathered face.

They continued beyond Blake's burial site for another five miles. Abruptly, the trail veered east and north.

Slocum reined Wind to a halt and examined the change, puzzled. Why would the rustlers head off the main trail? The herd had been destined for Dodge City, where the Atcheson, Topeka and Santa Fe Railroad would pick them up. The way the herd was headed now, it would cut across country and hit the Chisholm Trail, the trail Slocum had followed from Texas. Did the rustlers have a staging area somewhere to the northeast? Was it their intention to hit the Chisholm again, and go on to Ellsworth? The Kansas Pacific Railroad served Ellsworth and hauled cattle east to Kansas City. Were both ideas possible? Slocum concluded they were. A group of men bold enough to get away with five thousand longhorns in one giant swipe had it well planned.

As Slocum studied the situation, he came to a disheartening conclusion: There would be no way in which he could get his herd back. There had been at least a dozen men after the cattle the night before, and he knew there would be a crowd of reinforcements wherever the cattle eventually went. There would be a fight. His boys were in shock and angry, and they would fight hard, but did he want them to risk their lives? It was certain they would be outnumbered by a species of human being accustomed to killing and thievery, the outlaw breed. His men, for the most part young, would be daring and brave, and would probably end up dead. Slocum didn't want that. He liked his crew too much. Cattle were important, but men were more so.

He came out of his silent study of the situation, and said, "You men go back to the chuck wagon. I'm going on alone for a spell."

"Hell, no!" Curley exploded. "I want a piece of them people myself."

"You can't do it alone, boss," observed Rusty.

Except for Ken Dorsey, all of the men were Texans. They were fiercely loyal to each other, and believed in the old law of an eye for an eye. It was unacceptable that they should leave the death of friends personally unavenged.

"I understand how you feel," Slocum told them quietly, "but we're outnumbered, and you know it. We are going to have to wait for another time to even the score. For now, I want you to go back to the wagon. If I'm not with you by sundown, you are to continue to Dodge and report what happened to the marshal."

There was a sullen silence from his men. Slocum wondered if his authority would carry through this crisis. He sat straight in the saddle and eyed the crew steadily. As he did so, his hand brushed the rear of his cantle and touched a hole. That hole had not been present the day before. As he waited for his crew's reaction to his orders, he slipped a finger in the hole and bumped against a lump. He knew without looking that the lump was lead. Had not the cantle been so hard, of such tough leather, he would not have had to bother with women for the rest of his natural days. The bullet had travelled a long way, too, and was nearly spent when it reached him. He had been a lucky bastard last night. Very lucky.

Slocum was not an easy man. He was fair, but when he gave an order, he expected it to be carried out. It was his job to give orders on this drive. His crew hadn't shown any signs of agreeing. They wanted their revenge, and tension was building between himself and the men. He didn't want that. He didn't want trouble with a crew he respected, but he would not back down on his orders, either. The discipline of the trail had to be upheld, and Slocum was suddenly confronted with a grave problem.

The solution came to him as he fingered the small, round hole in his cantle.

He turned Wind so the men could see the hole.

"I nearly took one where I live last night," he said conversationally.

The men eyed the hole. They looked into Slocum's green eyes, at his solemn face, and back at the hole. They looked up again, and, as Slocum had hoped, one of the men, Blondy, broke into a grin.

"They almost made a capon outa you, boss," he observed.

The remark brought a soft chuckle from the others.

"Bobby would have cackled t' see that," said Rusty.

"Yeah. Yeah."

There were murmurs and smiles—sad smiles, but smiles—and the tension eased away.

"You men go back," Slocum said softly. "This is a one-man job, anyway. I just want to take a little look-see. Too many men, too much dust. Dust can be seen a long way."

"Yeah. All right."

Rusty touched his sombrero in salute. "We'll see you by sundown?"

Slocum nodded.

Rusty nodded and turned his horse down the back trail. The others followed.

"Get Blake's horse," Slocum said. "He's probably near the grave yet. We'll take him into Dodge."

Blondy waved in acknowledgment and the group galloped away. In moments they were lost in the rolling plains, and Slocum was alone. Maybe. Likely the rustlers had sent a man to the rear to watch their back trail. No need for him to tell his men that, but it was a thing a man learned on the trails he rode. When you think you're the only one around, it's time to step real careful. No, they had a man riding long drag, well in the rear. He already felt that eyes were watching him.

They were bad eyes.

3

Slocum had once been trailed by Chiricahua Apaches in the lower New Mexico desert. He was new to the country then, thirteen years before, and was en route to El Paso. The journey had been one of exploration, and he had had no particular goals in mind.

He did not have much in the way of wealth. The wealth of land that he and his family had once possessed in Georgia was gone. After the War, carpetbaggers swarmed over the South like maggots on rotten meat, and the family farm became grist for their mills of greed. Slocum had in self-defense shot and killed the Yankee judge who claimed the farm because of delinquent back taxes. Since a man couldn't shoot a judge—couldn't even nick him—Slocum had burned the farm buildings and left in a hurry. He had taken little with him, and he had never been back.

Slocum, even though he had been new to the Southwest —new to the entire West, in fact—realized the Chiricahuas wanted what little he had. Apaches didn't trail people

23

for the fun of it. They wanted his horse, another spotted bronc named Sparks, and his Texas saddle. They eyed his two Colt .31s, and his bedroll, too. If they guessed that there were gold sovereigns and some silver in his pockets, they would have been correct, and they would take the money, also. Lastly, they might have lifted his scalp. After all, a dead man hardly needed it, but it was great coup for them.

But Slocum, his senses and his instincts honed to a high degree after many night battles during the War, wasn't about to give the Apaches any of what they desired. He had stopped, drawn both pistols, and waited, hidden in a small but deep arroyo.

Within minutes three Chiricahuas appeared aboard scruffy-looking ponies, trotting swiftly. They were about to make their move.

"Hello," Slocum had called from his strategic hiding place.

The Indians slid to a halt and whirled to face their quarry. One levelled his Sharps carbine, a weapon probably taken from some white, and Slocum shot it out of his hand.

"Yow!" cried the Indian, whose fingers stung from the blow.

"I'll burn each one of you, if you don't head the other way fast!"

He fired again, and clipped the reins of another would-be robber. The man jerked in surprise and studied his sundered reins in wonder.

"I'll kill all of you," said Slocum quietly, "if I see you again."

The Apaches, their thick chests and squat bodies trembling with anger and humiliation, glared at Slocum. They would have charged, for they were fearless, and this white man had beaten them at their own game, which was unheard-of. But they were not foolish. The Colts pointed at them had shown their stuff. To charge would have been to greet the Great Spirit long before any of them desired. They turned their scraggy horses and left slowly, to show they weren't afraid.

"I'll be watching for you," Slocum had called after them. "Next time, I'll shoot all three of you dead."

He didn't know if they understood, but he thought they did. If the Indians didn't get the words, they got the tone, and tone was what counted. The tone was as deadly as Slocum could make it. Nor was he bluffing. One more confrontation, and there would have been a shootout. That was it.

As he rode along the rustled cattle's trail, Slocum recalled the incident. Apache eyes were no different from white eyes when their owners intended evil. One felt the fire just the same. Slocum had no doubt in his mind that they were white eyes that followed this time. They would belong to the rear guard of the crew that had taken his cattle.

Slocum didn't like playing follow the leader under these circumstances, so he stopped, just as he had for the Apaches in New Mexico. He waited, but he didn't hide. He wanted to be seen. He was using himself as bait to learn things that might be useful later—if he lived until later.

After a few minutes the eyes appeared. They belonged to four men, tough characters with narrow faces, two of them heavily moustached, all of them tanned and as hard as the saddle leather upon which they sat. They each wore a pistol and one carried a Henry repeating rifle.

They approached without a word until they were within twenty feet of Slocum. Then they stopped. They looked him over carefully, contemptuously. Then one spoke. He was a well-built man with a hawk face and a hank of brown hair showing below the brim of his hat.

"This here," he said icily, "is private property."

"I don't see any signs," returned Slocum, just as icily.

"You don't have to see any signs. I'm telling you. It's best to get off it, friend."

"I was heading to Ellsworth." Slocum nodded at the ground, which was blazed with the hooves of five thousand cattle. "Got an easy trail to follow here."

"You go another step and it'll be your last."

"Take it easy, Ord," said another of the men. "We don't want no more trouble than we can handle."

"Hell," snorted the man called Ord. "You call this stray saddletramp trouble?"

"The boss said no more killin'."

"To hell with what the boss said. I'm running this little party."

The wind had been coming from the southwest all morning, but was gradually making a change. It was now coming from the northwest, and it carried sounds. They were faint, but they were the unmistakable bellows of cattle. Slocum caught an odor, too, and he knew it to be branding irons at work. He was certain the Pollywog brand—the brand on the cattle he had been driving—was being changed. Somewhere in the distance there was a staging area, where his herd was being held. His herd, and perhaps others. He had learned what he wanted to know. It was time to leave.

"Well, then," he said, making his voice sound thin and scared, "I'll be heading back."

"Not so fast," said Ord.

Slocum sized him up. Unlike his companions, he carried two pistols. They looked heavy, Navy Colts, probably .44s. Or maybe they were Patersons. Slocum could not read them very well by their stocks. All he knew was that they were heavy guns, and the man who wore them was itching to make them speak. Slocum had a hunch the fellow had listened to their thunder before and wanted to hear it again. The man was a killer, probably a hired gun, maybe a regulator, and every now and then he had to kill somebody to prove his worth. Slocum sensed he was going to be the next target.

"No need for me to hang around," Slocum objected. "I

don't want trouble with you people."

"But you got it, Slocum," said Ord with a wicked grin.

Slocum was not surprised to hear his name. He had no doubt that Ord and the whole rotten bunch had known all about him, his men, and the cattle from a long way down the trail.

He dropped his pretense of fear. "Which one of you killed Ned Blake?" he asked.

The look of surprise that passed among the four was genuine, except for the man Ord. Slocum knew a liar when he saw one, and he was looking at an expert.

"Didn't you know it?" Slocum asked.

"Hell, no. He was supposed to . . ." Ord began. He was silenced by warning glances from the others.

"Well, somebody shot him," said Slocum. "Maybe one of my boys did it when you raided my cattle last night."

"We never took your cattle," said one of the four stoutly.

"I think you did."

"You'd have a devil of a time proving that."

"Are you calling us rustlers?" Ord interceded.

"Yes."

Slocum knew he was heading for trouble, but the anger and grief he had felt over Ken Dorsey's death was returning. It was compounded by the deaths of the two young cowboys who had, at this hour the day before, had their minds on women and Chinese food.

Ord went for his gun. He was fast. He was practiced in his trade. He was good, and he knew it, and he went for his right-hand gun. His hand dropped with the speed of a striking rattlesnake, a blur of action, and the heavy pistol was halfway out of its holster when the blur stopped suddenly. The owner of that very fast hand was looking into the deadly muzzle of Slocum's .31.

"Don't try it," said Slocum bitterly. "I'd just as soon blow your brains out as look at you."

The four were silent, all eyes on the pistol gripped in

Slocum's steady hand. He was never steadier than when
the pressure was on. It was on now.

"I've learned what I need to know," he said, "and you
can guess what it is. I don't hanker to kill any of you,
because I don't know if you took part in last night's butch-
ery. And there's no use in me going on any farther, because
I haven't the slightest doubt in my mind there are two
dozen more like you up ahead."

"I'll get you for this," growled Ord. "No man beats Ord
Wade to the draw."

"I did," Slocum reminded him, "and I will again if you
cause trouble. The next time, you'll never live to see the
muzzle of my friend, Judge Colt."

He turned Wind and headed along his own back trail.
He had had enough of Ord Wade and his band. He knew
what he wanted to know, and he realized there was nothing
he could do about it now. Sometimes a minute of "shut-up"
was worth five years of a man's life. The man who lived
long was the man who picked the time and place for a
gunfight, not the one who let himself get drawn into a
fracas. He had been outgunned, pure and simple. Anything
could happen in such a situation. A busted cap could jam
in the wheel and stop the cylinder cold. A pistol at such
times wasn't any more use than a club, and a club didn't
stand much chance against a bullet.

"Don't follow," he called. "I'll kill the first one of you
that I see."

He put Wind into a steady, mile-eating gallop. He
passed the stony grave of Ned Blake, and wondered at the
surprise the men had shown when he mentioned Blake's
death. They apparently hadn't known he'd been hit, though
he was pretty sure Wade knew something. There was less
doubt than ever, now, that Blake had been mixed up in
this. That led to another question: How about Earl Blake?
Did he fit into the scheme of things, too? Yes, what about
his partner, Earl?

He made it back to the chuck wagon long before dark,

taking care that he hadn't been followed. Evidently, Wade and his men had taken his warning seriously, because he hadn't seen them again. On the other hand, they probably had more important things to do than chase after him, such as help change the Pollywog brand on five thousand head of longhorns.

Slocum's men were glad to see him back.

"I was about to come lookin'," Rusty admitted.

"I said to wait until sundown," Slocum reminded him, "then go to Dodge."

"We was worried anyway," said Blondy.

Slocum nodded. That would be like the crew. They were concerned about him and would disobey orders if they thought his safety was jeopardized. It was all right.

"You hungry?" Cooky asked.

Slocum shook his head. He noted that a large grave had been dug and the bodies of Ken, Bobby, and Tubby had been wrapped in tarps and laid side by side. Each man's possessions lay on top of his body, to be buried with him, except for the weapons they owned. Weapons were too hard to come by, and would be inherited by the survivors. Though Slocum hated the thought, it was likely that Indians would dig up the grave and rob it. If they found weapons, they could be used against whites in the continuous warfare between the two races.

"Let's get on with it," he said.

Grabbing a shovel, he poured dirt over the bodies, not liking the soft splashing sound it made hitting the tarps. He pursed his lips into determined lines and continued to shovel. He had tended many burial details during the War. This was not new to him, but it was poignant, and his heart was heavy. Three good men gone for greed. Useless! At least in the War a man had died for a cause. What was the cause here? Greed! Some son of a bitch wanted his cattle for free, and he killed three innocent men to get them. Slocum made a vow as he shoveled, and sweat from the effort popped out on his brow: He would find the men who had caused last night's action. He had no doubt that Ord Wade was one, but he was small potatoes. There were some bigger people in this somewhere, and they were the ones Slocum wanted.

After the last shovel of dirt had been dropped into place, Slocum and the others stood by the grave silently. There was no Bible at hand, but Slocum felt the need to say something, speak a farewell to those whom he would never hear or see again.

"I guess," he began quietly, "we all live and we will all die. It is a law of life that death follows. But we wish that God had seen fit for you men, our friends, to stick around a little while longer. You were good to us, and for us, and we will miss you. . . . Amen."

There was a murmur of "Amens" from the others. Then Slocum turned to Cooky.

"Hitch up," he said, "and let's go. There's nothing more we can do here."

But there was plenty to be done in the future. Somebody had stolen his herd. Who was behind it? Somebody had cost the lives of three fine men, and somebody was going to pay for that, too. Somebody would pay.

4

The grave had been marked with three crude crosses of weathered planking torn from the chuck wagon. Rusty had carved the names of the men on the crosspieces.

"Indians will know what's under them crosses for sure," objected one of the crew, a lanky Texan they called Boots. His real name was Reginald Bollinger, but no one had called him by either of those names in many years.

"They know it anyways," grunted Rusty. "You think we ain't bein' watched?"

Slocum knew that Rusty was right. Where there were large herds of cattle, you would probably find Indians begging for a steer. They knew of last night's raid, and they knew of the deaths. They would know of the grave, marked or unmarked.

He ended the discussion. "Let's go."

Cooky put the chuck wagon into motion.

They camped ten miles from the scene of the tragedy that night. Slocum posted a guard just to make sure neither

Indians nor whites attempted trouble. Wade might not have followed him that day, but Slocum was taking no chances.

It seemed odd not to have five thousand head of cattle milling nearby. Their grunts, groans, and outright bawls had accompanied him for a thousand miles. He had grown accustomed to the racket, had in fact been reassured by it, for a noisy herd was a herd in the right place—near him.

The silence was deafening. He had heard the expression before, and during the war had learned its meaning after a fierce battle. Tonight the silence was especially telling. It meant that he had failed as a trail boss, for one thing. He would be held responsible for the loss of the herd, whether it was his fault or not. He wouldn't be punished, and he would receive his pay, though not the percentage he had counted on. That end of it would be all right. But his reputation would have been damaged. A trail boss could lose a few cattle to rustlers. It was almost expected that there would be losses. But to let five thousand longhorns slip through his fingers? There wasn't a rancher or a buyer in the West who would trust him again.

Slocum let out a heavy sigh. He would have to find the lost herd and bring them back to Dodge to save his reputation, and how was he going to do that? One man against two dozen didn't have much of a chance. And by the time he got into action, the brands would be changed. There was a way to prove they had been changed, but hell, the cattle were probably already headed for the holding pens at Ellsworth. A good part of them, at least, and by the time he got back on the trail a week from now, they would all be gone.

He hadn't eaten all day, and for the first time he felt hunger. He paid a visit to the chuck wagon, and Cooky, who bunked under it, got up and fixed him a meal of cold beans, bread, and a slab of dried-apple pie. He washed it down with hot coffee. There was always a pot of coffee sitting near the fire.

It was a silent camp. The men were tired, and they

missed their companions, who less than twenty-four hours
before had been joking about what they would do in
Dodge. Slocum selected himself to relieve the guard at
midnight, and Rusty would relieve him at four. They
would head for Dodge by six. It was a three-day trip from
where they now were—less if they pushed—and Slocum
suddenly found himself wanting to push. He wanted to face
Earl Blake and then get on with the business he had in
mind. He was going to find the killers of his friends. That
was first, and when he did that, he would automatically
learn who rustled his herd. Maybe he could salvage his
reputation.

They reached Dodge at noon on the third day. Dodge
was booming. The holding pens were full of cattle; the
streets were full of men and women. The women who were
visible belonged to the families of the settlers. Kansas was
a growing farm region, and homesteaders was pouring into
the area. Wheat was the big crop, and with the arrival of
trains, shipping was practical.

The women he saw didn't interest Slocum. What he
wanted from a woman, none of these would willingly give.
His goal would be what were happily called "nymphs of
the prairie," and they inhabited a section of Dodge south of
the Santa Fe tracks. If you saw a man bowlegging in that
direction, you knew he wasn't shopping for groceries. Of
course, there were girls in the saloons who could supply
the same product, and Slocum, whose boundaries were
flexible, might purchase an evening from one of them. Or
an entire night, the way he felt.

Though they had no cattle, Slocum headed for the pens
and parked the chuck wagon. Next, he paid the men from a
payroll that had been entrusted to him when the drive
began. It was money for expenses along the way, and to
cash out any cowboy who wanted to quit the drive.

"What you goin' to do?" Rusty asked.

"I have to see Earl Blake. Then I'm heading back to
where we lost the cattle," Slocum told him.

Rusty's eyes flickered. "We want to go with you." He glanced at a saloon. "First, mebbe, we'd like to wash this dust out of our throats."

"I won't be leaving before daylight tomorrow, but I'd advise any of you against coming along."

"Why's that?" asked Curley.

"You know why," Slocum said evenly. "It might get bloody."

"You think we don't know that?" demanded Boots, the man with the elegant footwear. "We know it, boss."

The others murmured agreement. They didn't care about the blood. They were Texans, and they were after some people who killed their friends. It was a matter of loyalty and honor. No Northern bastard was going to kill their own and get away with it.

Slocum was sure that if they didn't all go together, his crew would head out on their own. He understood men like Ord Wade. At times in his life, he had been an Ord Wade. His crew, except for Rusty, maybe, and Cooky, didn't know what kind of a man they were up against. It would be a slaughter. Better they go on the trail together. At least he might keep some of them from getting killed.

"Meet me in front of the Long Branch at five," he said.

The men doffed their hats, a sign of agreement, then rode off to touch, taste, and fondle the pleasures Dodge offered.

Slocum put Wind in a stable and headed for the Dodge House. It was a sizable hotel where buyers turned their cash into beef. Earl Blake stayed there when he was in Dodge. Slocum wasn't sure how Blake was going to take the news about the loss of his herd. Actually, the loss shouldn't bother his partner all that much, except as a matter of inconvenience. As far as Slocum knew, Blake hadn't paid for the cattle yet. They were C.O.D., and he had only arranged for their delivery. No buyer would pay for a herd before it reached a railhead. There were too many chances for loss on a thousand-mile journey. Slocum would take the loss on this deal. He would get his salary but no percentage.

As for Blake's loss of his brother, Ned—well, every man had to take a loss of somebody close now and then. Slocum had lost his older brother in the War, and he still felt the loss. Blake would just have to take it. It was a tough thing to have to tell a man, though, that his brother was dead, shot down by rustlers. John shivered as his boots rang on the boardwalk.

Slocum mounted the steps of the Dodge House's veranda. As he did so, Earl Blake stepped out. He was followed by Ord Wade and several tough-looking men. One of them had his arm in a sling.

"Hello, Earl," said Slocum. "I'll just bet you've heard about the cattle."

"You son of a bitch," said Earl Blake bitterly. "You bastard."

Blake was the opposite of his brother, Ned. Ned had been skinny; Earl Blake was not. He wasn't fat, he was just damned big. What a polite man might call large. He had a barrel chest and his head seemed to have been plunked right down on top of it. No neck was visible. His arms were those of a professional strongman. His biceps stretched his jacket tight, and his thighs were as thick as bridge beams. He was well dressed, and a sixgun hung low on his hip.

Slocum had not been prepared for an open-arms greeting, but he hadn't expected such anger either. He flushed and his eyes grew steely. "Whoa," he said softly. "I don't think I rate that, Earl."

"My brother knew what you were up to and you killed him," Blake growled. "You shot him dead. I got the body in the morgue to prove it."

"Wasn't my weapon that downed your brother," said Slocum. "That's easily proved."

"Maybe you didn't pull the trigger," said Blake, "but one of your men did."

"We never killed Ned," said Slocum. "I don't know who did. And I never rustled your cattle." He pointed at Ord Wade. "He did."

Wade stiffened, but Blake shook his head. He wasn't ready for a showdown yet.

Slocum pushed it. "Your killer boys brought you the news pretty fast."

"They found Ned on the trail and brought him in to Dodge. They could pretty well figure out what happened. They saw you heading toward Ellsworth with the herd."

"They've been busy," said Slocum pleasantly. He nodded toward the man with his arm in a sling. "How'd you get that?" he asked. "Somebody shoot you the night you took my cattle?"

"You did it, didn't you?" was the hot retort. "I saw you shootin' at me—"

Ord Wade brought the edge of his hand down on the man's wound. The blow brought a cry of pain, and a hissed warning from Wade.

"Shut up, you jackass. You'll get more than a bullet in the arm if you don't."

"See?" Slocum was smiling. He addressed Blake. "Your boys weren't just passing by, were they? At midnight? What's up, Blake? Did you have Ned shot because he knew too much? What's your game? Couldn't you trust that skinny brother of yours? He was the one who gave the signal to your boys that the time was ripe for a strike, wasn't he?"

"*You* had him killed," roared Earl Blake, "and by God you're going to pay."

"Does this mean our partnership is over, Blake?"

"Well, for Christ's sake, what do you think?"

"I think you owe me three months' wages. I'll let the percentage of the cattle sale go until I find the herd."

Slocum's every sense was alert. He knew he was walking on quicksand. If he stepped too heavy he would go down. He might get Ord and one or two others, but Blake had plenty of men grouped around, all hardcases. They would know what to do and do it. Slocum knew he'd be dead before he could squeeze off his fourth shot. The smile he was using was a phony one, put on to irritate Blake. Under the smile, under his pleasant manner, he was furious. He knew he had been tricked, that Blake had used him, and Slocum didn't like being used. He had brought the cattle a thousand miles and walked right into a trap.

"Your brother," he said gently, "must have stunk pretty bad, if they brought him in. Three days in this Kansas heat? Of course, your brother was nothing but shoelaces and bone, anyway. Nothing there to stink."

Earl Blake glared. "Why, you heartless son of a bitch," he sputtered. "Give me them saddlebags."

Slocum had brought the bags with what was left of the money. They also held the paperwork on the herd. He had them slung over his shoulder, and he let them down on his forearm, then deftly unbuckled one. It held the money.

"I'll just take my pay first," he said.

"Like hell . . ."

Slocum's .31 appeared, pointed and cocked. "Don't make me mess up your pretty clothes," said Slocum. "All I want is my pay."

He extracted a number of coins, gold and silver, and pocketed them. Then he dropped the bags.

"Get him," Blake roared at Wade. "He's robbing me."

Even Ord Wade, a gunman practiced in the art of drawing fast, blinked at that order.

"He tries it and he's dead," said Slocum, still pleasantly, but then his voice hardened. "Listen, Blake—listen, all of you." His eyes bored into Wade's. "I lost three good men in that raid. They should never have died. I'm going to find out who caused that raid, and then I'm going to settle with him."

"You'll hang first!" cried Blake, raging. "You killed my brother, and you'll hang for it!"

Slocum backed off, keeping his Colt leveled steadily at

the group on the Dodge House's veranda. A curious crowd had gathered in the street.

"Stop him!" cried Blake. "A thousand dollars to the man who shoots him."

Slocum faced the crowd, keeping an eye on the veranda as well.

"Hell, that's John Slocum," came a voice from the onlookers. "I seen him in action in El Paso once. He left two dead, and three wishin' they was."

"Yeah, said another. "I saw him clean out a bar with his fists in San Antonio. They was ten to one, and he knocked every one of 'em silly."

Over the years since his arrival in the West, John Slocum had gained some fame and notoriety. What was known about him mattered in a country where guns and fists often meant the right to keep on living. Not all of the crowd knew about John Slocum, but some did, and their knowledge was enough to stay the hands of those who might try.

Slocum slipped through the crowd without hindrance, then ran like hell for Wind. He slapped his saddle on the startled horse and lit out just as Blake and Wade showed up. Slocum fired over their heads and they ducked. He urged Wind to a full run, but shots followed him down the street. He heard lead whistle overhead and chunk into the posts holding up porches. It was close, but he had learned one thing in the dangerous life he led: As long as you are moving, keep moving and never stop.

"Come on, boy," he shouted to Wind, "let's head for the plains and get lost."

He left town at top speed and rode swiftly for a mile, glancing back every now and then to see if there were pursuers. There weren't, but there would be. He was sure of that. Earl Blake wanted him dead. It was now about three o'clock in the afternoon. Four more hours till darkness. He cursed. Why couldn't this have all happened later in the afternoon? He would be a clay pigeon for a posse. Though Wind was fast and had great endurance, he couldn't keep up the pace for long. Something had to be done.

John let the idea grow. He knew he was in a tough spot, but his back wasn't to the wall yet. And then it struck him. He was running like a scared jackrabbit, right out in the open where he was an easy target. That was what they would expect him to do. And it was the wrong thing to do. But what was the right thing?

It was no more than a hunch, but Slocum trusted his hunches. He turned Wind north and then back west again, back toward Dodge. He was doubtful if a posse would pick up his tracks. The area was a jumble of tracks of both cattle and horses. They would be looking for him, for his horse, for a spot of dust on the horizon. They would be looking for him out in the open, running like a stone-brained rabbit.

He circled back north of town and found a deep gully. He dismounted and, holding onto Wind's reins, sat on the ground and listened. He listened all that afternoon, but nobody ever came close. His ruse had worked, and after darkness fell, he felt better. He was safe for a while.

For a while, but for how long? Blake packed a lot of influence in the right, high places of Dodge. He was a power, and he had just made John Slocum an outlaw. If John Slocum were to show his face in Dodge, he would be a dead man. He had to find out what was going on, why Blake accused him of rustling. After that he had to prove that Blake was a liar. That wasn't going to be easy.

Everyone in Dodge seemed to know Blake and respect him.

Nobody knew Slocum from Adam.

Except those who wanted him dead.

5

As John Slocum squatted in the dark next to Wind, he grinned ruefully. The plan took slow shape in his mind, grew out of the darkness of the night. He would get no justice in Dodge. Boot Hill was thick with men who had gotten none long before he set foot in that lawless excuse for a town. There was a better way. The cattle weren't in Dodge. He knew that. When the herd's trail had swung off, he had known it. And he didn't see a damned thing in the pens he recognized. No; the cattle were somewhere else, and if he reckoned right, they had not gone to Hays.

He made up his mind, then. He was going to Ellsworth to prove his innocence. He was going to bring the men who had caused the death of his friends to justice—his own justice or the law's. Ellsworth was a six-day trip from Dodge by horse. Less, if he pushed.

Now the doubts began to creep in and chip chinks off his resolve. What in hell did he plan to do for food along the way? Eat grass like Wind? He had left his bedroll at the

41

stable. Would he sleep in a prairie-dog hole? Ride all the way without sleep? Slocum grunted in disgust. He had to have food, and he needed at least one blanket. There was only one place to get them, and that place was Dodge. He was now a wanted man in Dodge, so how would he get his supplies?

There were three options: he could find one of the boys —Curley, maybe, or Rusty would be better—and have him get the supplies. But locating them would mean he would have to enter the saloons of Dodge. A wanted man in a well-lit place was a fool looking for a cell—or a noosed rope.

He could look up Ken Dorsey's sister, Marisa. She ran a seamstress shop in her home, and Ken had told Slocum where it was. Slocum had meant to see her anyway, to convey the news of Ken's death, along with his personal regrets. He had planned to give her Ken's wages, too, because a seamstress in Dodge probably didn't exactly live high on the hog. When Slocum had taken the money from the saddlebags, he had extracted Ken's wages as well. Blake would never have bothered to pay Ken's sister. He didn't even know who was in the crew.

Should he look up Marisa? Should he present himself at her door, after dark, with the news of her brother's death, and then ask for help? Wasn't there the possibility of somebody seeing him? Dodge was a restless town. It was a late-night town, particularly when the big cattle drives came in. People walked here and there, and someone could very well run into him. That wouldn't do Marisa the slightest bit of good. No. Plan number two was a flop. He would see Marisa with his condolences and Ken's wages, but that would have to come later, after things had cooled off.

There was only one choice left. He would have to commit a break-in. He would find a general store and take what he needed.

Slocum studied the night sky. There would be a moon

later, but right now the stars were the only illumination. The less light the better. He knew where to go. Slocum knew Dodge City well. He had spent the finish of several cattle drives in Dodge. He had also once served as a deputy marshal under Ed Masterson. For six months he had patrolled the streets of Dodge, and he knew where all the right doors were.

He mounted Wind and rode toward the city's lights. Within half an hour he was close enough to hear the tinny music, the shouts and laughter of cowboys glad their own thousand-mile treks were over. Mingled with this were the more calculated shrieks of delight from women of the night. Slocum had noticed the frantic falseness of soiled doves before. No matter where they plied their trade, in saloons or red-light districts, for them bedding a man was business. Tonight, removed as he was from the center of hearty gaiety, the difference between genuine laughter and the calculated hilarity of a woman on the commercial prowl was pronounced. Again he grinned ruefully. He was between a rock and a hard place, and the usual business of the town was not his concern this night.

Slocum left Wind ground-tied in the shadows at the edge of town, and followed the alleys and back paths past the outhouses and cisterns. When he came to a certain building, he tested the door. Naturally, it was locked. Slocum knew how to handle locked doors, especially those made from the flimsy material in this building. He raised a booted foot and kicked it hard just once, right by the knob, and the door popped open.

As noisy as Dodge might be, such sounds, coming from a dark alley, could cause attention. There might be deputies roaming, as he once had. Slocum ducked between two buildings and waited. After several moments, he judged the way to be clear and entered the building. He closed the door after him and jammed a chair under the knob, just in case the law came by.

The place was faintly lit by the spill of yellow light from

the kerosene lamps hanging outside two saloons across the street. It wasn't much light, but enough for Slocum to make his choices in a hurry—canned peaches, canned tomatoes, bacon, hardtack, coffee, a frying pan for the bacon, and pot for the coffee. He found two wool blankets, a tarp, and some extra clothes, and stuffed the entire swag into a gunny sack.

As he was leaving, his eyes fell on the cigar counter near the front of the store. He set his sack down and tiptoed over to the counter. His eyes sparkled with interest as they assessed the cigars. Havanas, his favorite cigars. Alongside the Havanas were lesser smokes, the ten-for-a-quarter kind. Slocum had had his share of both, depending on how much money he had. He greatly preferred the Havanas, and he helped himself to an entire box. It was going to be a rough trip, so he might as well have some comforts. He would leave Dodge still dirty from the trail, and still womanless, but at least he would have a good cigar.

He laid a gold coin near the cash register to pay for his plunder and was about to leave when Earl Blake, Ord Wade, and another man appeared in front of the window. Slocum ducked. It wasn't likely they could see him in the dim light, but he wasn't taking any chances.

He took off his wide-brimmed Stetson to make his outline less conspicuous and raised his head for a look. The three men had stopped and were talking among themselves. Blake was waving his arms, and Slocum could hear words, if not whole sentences.

"Went . . . don't think he . . . get him!"

Ord Wade pointed once in the direction Slocum had taken when he raced out of town.

The third man appearred to be listening. He was a tall man clad in a gray business suit. He wore no hat, and gray hair topped his thin face with its high, aristocratic nose. There was something cruel and ruthless about the face. The face reflected the inner spirit of the man, perhaps, the absolute hardness of his core. His manner seemed relaxed, but even from where he crouched, Slocum could tell the man was tight with anger and tension.

When this man spoke, the others listened. When he gestured, the others watched his hands to get their meaning. He was the leader of the three, Slocum was certain. Both Blake and Wade were in the process of justifying an action, probably the loss of a certain trail boss, Slocum guessed. But the third man was having none of their excuses. His cruel face hardened, and when he spoke his lips scarcely moved. He turned once, and spat contemptuously into the street, then glared a gesticulating Blake into silence. Even the killer, Ord Wade, seemed to shrink back. Whatever it was about, the man was giving them hell, and they were taking it.

Slocum admired the man for dressing the two down, but he also realized that the man would be his enemy. If they ever fought, there would be no quarter.

Slocum considered his present advantage. He would probably never have a better opportunity to gun down two men who were his enemies. He could down Blake and then swing to Wade before the gunman could gather his wits. By ambushing the pair, Slocum's troubles in Dodge would become less pressing. Without Blake to keep people inflamed, chances were they would forget about Slocum. But if he killed Blake and Wade, he would have to kill the third man as well. Dead men didn't talk. Yet he didn't really know if the man was his enemy, did he? He only suspected it because of the company he kept.

Slocum sighed. He could never cut anybody down by bushwhacking them. He had done it during the War, because that was his job, but he came away from the War hating what he had had to do. Any man Slocum had fought since that time had been a fair fight in the open.

He tiptoed back to where his sack of supplies lay. Picking it up, he watched the three by the front window until they moved on. He let out a breath and wiped sweat from his forehead. The ache in his shoulders as he hefted the sack told him he needed rest. He looked around one more time. There was nothing more he needed here. Slocum made his way out of the empty store without incident. He found Wind, loaded his saddlebags with his goods, tied his bedroll in place, and moved on. He would ride all night and sleep during the day. That way there was less chance of being seen by hostile eyes. The moon would give sufficient light, and the trail was not difficult to follow.

For three nights, Slocum followed his own back trail out of Dodge. When he came to the point where the rustlers had turned northeast, he took that route. However, he rode some distance from the trail, going by landmarks. He doubted if Wade and his boys would be around, but other guards were probably posted. A hill higher than the others was his guide. It was near the hill where he had heard the cattle in the distance before he had been turned back by armed men. As long as he kept the hill in sight, and remained a good distance from the main trail, he felt safe.

When the hill paralleled him, he closed in, heading in a northeasterly direction. His calculations proved correct, because he covered only two miles before he spotted the cattle. There were probably at least ten thousand beeves milling around. There was no doubt in Slocum's mind that this was a staging area for the cattle thieves. Brands were altered here. After that, the animals were driven to Ellsworth, or perhaps Hays, on the Kansas Pacific Railroad track.

The place was ideal. Far from the main trails, it wasn't likely to be discovered by unwanted eyes such as his.

Slocum was going to pass on by. The chances of his getting near enough to see the cattle up close and prove his suspicions were small. But as he urged Wind in the direction of the Chisholm Trail some miles east, he stopped. If he saw just one of his cattle in the bunch, it would be all the proof he needed in his own mind. He would then be certain. As it stood, he only had suspicions. True, he was ninety-nine percent sure, but that one percent still cast a shadow of a doubt. Even if he saw his Pollywog brand, he would never be able to prove anything. Blake was too powerful. Money talked, and money could buy silence as well. It could silence a hundred witnesses. Lead also had a way of doing that, and Slocum wouldn't put it past Blake to use lead if he found it necessary.

He studied the situation in his mind. It would be worth the risk to take a closer look, but there was considerable danger in the enterprise. A nearly full moon lit the countryside like a giant round candle. He and Wind stood out like raisins in rice. If he was caught, he would be shot right then, because he was sure that he was known to at least some of the men, and they had their orders. Or he might be taken back to Dodge, where Blake and Ord Wade would have the satisfaction of seeing him hang. And that third man Slocum had seen outside the store—would he be pleased by a hanging? Possibly.

Slocum grinned without mirth. He had it in him to make plenty of folks feel good, but it was the wrong way, and for the wrong folks.

"Wind," he said, "you stay here. I got to do a bit of foot travel."

He dismounted and ran swiftly toward the cattle. He could see riders slowly circling the herd, night guards. Though rustled, there was nothing to keep these critters from acting just like ordinary cattle. They could spook at a storm and run. They could spook for no reason on earth and run to hell and gone, so nightriders were necessary.

In the soft whisper of air, along with the grunts and moans from the herd, Slocum heard faint singing. The guards, who were probably innocent cowboys for the most part in need of a little extra cash, were crooning lullabies to soothe the animals. The songs also gave away their position as they rode, and Slocum paid heed. Even though the moon was bright enough to read a newspaper by, it wasn't easy to distinguish the guards. Their horses' outlines were blotted against those of the cattle, and they all looked much the same.

Bobbing and weaving, he closed in on the herd. Once a guard passed within two hundred feet of him, and he froze. He kept his face down to keep the white skin from showing, and made himself look as much like one of the boulders in the landscape as possible. The guard continued without any idea that his death had been a finger twitch away, because Slocum's hand was on the butt of his Colt.

Carefully, skillfully, Slocum drew close to the herd. Most were lying down, but a few were standing, and he concentrated on these. He didn't penetrate the herd, not wanting to risk it on foot. His presence on foot could have caused a panic or at least excitement, which would bring a guard to see what was happening. A rider was accepted by cattle, but a man on foot was a strange thing, a threatening intruder, and the cattle, half-wild beasts that they were, took the direct route in ridding themselves of the danger. Many a luckless man had been gored while on foot.

The brands were difficult to see in spite of the moonlight. Slocum drew in closer. He had to know. Then he saw a Pollywog. It was unmistakable. The Pollywog brand lay sideways, an easy brand to recognize.

Damn! Slocum was pleased. There was the positive proof he needed. At least any doubt had now vanished in his own mind. He knew he would never get the law to believe him. Even if he did, the Pollywog brands would have been obliterated or changed by then. He tried to see other brands, and thought he saw a square "U" on one, when a voice interrupted his consideration.

"What you doin' there, fella?"

Slocum turned quickly to see a young cowboy approaching on his mount.

Slocum's brains meshed into gear at once.

"Why," he said, "I'm heeding mother nature, friend."

"What you mean?" demanded the cowboy.

Slocum pretended to be buttoning his pants. "Can't you guess?"

"Oh—oh, yeah, I get it." The cowboy's mount was now close. "Listen, we got to get the branding finished up by first light and head this bunch to Ellsworth. You better turn in or you won't be worth a tinker's damn come sunup."

"I'm new here. Just got in today."

"Oh, yeah? I don't recollect any new people today." The voice was edged with suspicion. "Say, who are you, anyway?"

While the conversation was taking place, Slocum had sidled up to the guard's horse. Just as the last question came out, Slocum was within striking distance, and strike he did. He reached up and grabbed an arm and pulled. The cowboy tumbled off his mount, landing with a crash on the hard ground. The man opened his mouth to cry out. Slocum brought the butt of his Colt smashing down on the man's head, and the struggling figure collapsed. Without hesitation, Slocum climbed aboard the guard's mount, and continued the circuit as if nothing had happened. The cowhand lay still. He would be out for a while. Slocum rode out a ways from the herd. Then he dismounted and, making himself as small as possible, ran for Wind. It was better to go on foot. If the other guards saw a horse galloping away, their suspicions would immediately prompt them to follow.

Slocum reached Wind as out of breath as he had ever been in his life. His throat and lungs burned as if they had been coated with kerosene and set on fire. He set Wind into motion, riding slowly, as if he had not a care in the world. Once he stopped and looked back. All was calm. The young guard's horse waited where he had left him, but it wouldn't be long before the unconscious Texan would come to. Then there would be particular hell raised, but by then, Slocum would have put distance between them.

It wasn't too far from there to Chisholm. Slocum was

on it by daylight. He stopped for coffee and some hardtack and then kept going. It didn't matter if he travelled by day now. He was far enough from Dodge that it was doubtful a posse would reach him. He met many people on the trail, ranging from cowboys on their way to Dodge or heading back to Texas to settlers with their wagons of possessions. None knew him, and he wanted to get to Ellsworth pronto. The next step was to see if his cattle were being shipped and what the brand had been changed to by the rustlers. He would have liked to have gotten his hands on one of the running irons and used that for proof, but maybe it was just as well he hadn't. He was in enough trouble. In cattle country, a man caught with a running iron was considered a rustler. Honest cattlemen just strung such men up to the nearest cottonwood tree, no questions asked.

Suddenly, Slocum realized how tough it was going to be. These rustlers were well organized. They held all the aces. They even owned the deck.

Could it be? He wondered.

Something slid in his stomach, something oily and sickening that made him queasy.

Maybe, he thought, these were not ordinary rustlers at all, but good men gone wrong, for whatever reason—greed, blood feuds.

Not ordinary rustlers at all, but cattlemen.

Slocum dug his spurs into Wind's flanks. His eyes narrowed to slits and a muscle rippled along his jawline.

For the first time, he realized how big a chunk he had bitten off to chew.

6

Ellsworth was not so large as Dodge City, but it had everything Dodge had, from loading pens to a red-light district.
The district was called Nauchville, and was easily found. It
was, Slocum thought ironically, probably the safest place
to be for a man on the dodge. The law stayed out of the
brothels except under the most extreme circumstances. It
was as if the town had set aside a place for sinning, and as
long as the people in Nauchville stayed to themselves, it
was all right.

It was early evening, and shadows stretched across the
dusty street. Though it was not likely he would be recognized, Slocum kept his face lowered. Some of Blake's
men, perhaps even some of those who had done the actual
rustling, could be holed up in Ellsworth. Slocum was taking no chances.

He went to the stockyards first, and circled them, eyeing the beef. There were all kinds of brands visible, including some from big ranches like the Running W, the

51

Rocking 7, and the Slash. Half a dozen brands were present, but Slocum could find no Pollywog cows. Was it possible they had been sent to Hays, or even Abilene? The idea was not encouraging, and Slocum's frustration increased. He had come a long way for nothing. One thing he was sure about: The thieves would get rid of the cattle as quickly as they could. There was risk in keeping them, since discovery was always possible. More than one Western hanging tree attested to that.

Slocum was just about to head for a hotel when a brand caught his eye. It looked like the Pollywog, but there was another circle on the end of the tail.

He stared hard at the brand, realizing that the right-hand circle could have been burned in recently. Whoever had performed the job had been skilled. He had burned the hair only. After a few days' drive over the Kansas prairie had dustied and dirtied the altered mark, it was difficult to tell that the mark was of recent manufacture. No buyer was going to question it. No buyer really cared. With beef prices up in the East, all such men wanted was cattle.

Slocum set astride Wind, looking at the altered brand with growing anger. It was as if that goddamned running iron had wiped out a thousand miles of sweat and the blood of good men. He felt as if he and the men who rode with him had lost more than time, more than the hard miles. They had lost pride in a job well done, the satisfaction of delivering a herd to railhead. Earl Blake, of course, would lose nothing. He would gain a thousandfold, perhaps more.

"Got yer eyes stuck, mister?" a voice intruded.

Slocum turned toward the sound of the voice. An old cowhand sat astride a moth-eaten, seedy cow pony, eyeing Slocum with unforgiving cynicism. It was as if he knew exactly what Slocum was looking for. Slocum sensed this, and forged ahead with a question of his own.

"What brand is that?" Slocum asked, pointing.

"Why, that's the Rolling Log mark. Ain't you never heard of that one?"

"Nope."

"Well, neither have I, till a few days back. They been shippin' 'em out of here by the hunnerts, though."

"Who do they belong to?"

The old man's flinty eyes sparked with suspicion.

"How in hell would I know? I just prod 'em on the cars. Don't make no difference t' me who they belong to, mister."

Whether the man knew or not, Slocum was sure he wasn't going to admit it. The only certain way to find out was to see a shipping manifest. The manifest would state who the cows belonged to and where they were destined. How to get the manifest? It probably lay in the shipping office, which was a large two-storied building some distance from the pens. Close enough to be handy, far enough to be away from most of the smell.

"Fair enough," said Slocum, turning his horse. The old man watched him, snorted, and shook his head.

Slocum trotted Wind over and dismounted. He went in. The door had a spring tying it to the wall; it smacked shut with a sound like a thunderclap. There was only one man in the office, the evening shipping clerk. His eyes were hidden under a green eyeshade, and he was bent over a pile of papers.

Without looking up, he asked, "Yes, what is it?"

It was the sort of paperwork insolence that Slocum abhorred. It said, *I'm just too busy for you, kindly don't bother me at such important work.*

"Look at me," Slocum snapped. He wanted to reach across the desk and cuff the man with the back of his hand.

The clerk looked up, startled. When he saw the fury in Slocum's fiery eyes, he set his pen down quickly. His face, pale from indoor work, turned to putty white.

"S-sorry," he stuttered, "I've just got so much to do . . ."

"I like to see a man's eyes when I talk to him. Some information, if you please. I want to know who is shipping the Rolling Log cattle?"

"I can't give that information out."

"Now, why in hell not? Maybe I've got a deal for the owner." Slocum's fury began to ebb, but there was still that lone muscle twitching along his jawline. The man presented such a pitiful figure that pity was replacing anger. Slocum knew he could never rough the man up. The fellow was doing what he thought was his job. But Slocum had to know who was shipping the Rolling Log, so he bluffed.

"Give me them manifests," he ordered, pointing at the pile of paper the clerk had been working on. "You can say, if you are ever asked, that you were forced into it."

Without a word, the clerk handed Slocum the papers. John thumbed through them quickly and found what he wanted. The manifest marked "Rolling Log" carried Earl Blake's name as shipper. The cattle were destined for Armour in Chicago.

All Slocum really needed was Blake's name. Now he had it. He knew who was behind the rustling. There was no doubt. Yet he still had no proof except in his own mind, because, after all, who was to say Rolling Log was not a genuine brand? If Blake was really as smart as he appeared to be, he could probably produce bills of sale for every head of beef. The only way to tell for sure if those brands had been altered was to kill one of the cows and strip its hide, then look underneath the brand. The old brand would be there, intact as the day it was burned in.

That was the one facet to the puzzle that bothered him. Was Earl Blake really smart enough to put this large a scheme together all by himself? True, the man was clever —slick might be a better word. He had, after all, managed to make John Slocum out as a crook. That took cleverness. But was he resourceful enough to pull off an operation this size?

Slocum tossed the papers back on the clerk's desk.

"Thanks," he growled, then turned on his heel and stalked out, his boot heels sounding like thunder as the door clapped shut once more.

He put Wind up in the livery stable, making sure his saddle was ready to throw on at a moment's notice, and he parked his bedroll beside it. He wasn't known in Ellsworth, but that had been half an hour ago. Now two men knew him: the cowpoke and the clerk. They would say something to somebody and start forces rolling that would not be favorable to John Slocum.

He walked to a hotel, carrying his saddlebags, keeping to the shadows, his hatbrim pulled down over his face. He checked into a dollar-a-night fleabag called Trail's End Inn, paid the wizened clerk, signed "John Smith" on the register, and took the key to his room upstairs. He lay down on the bed to rest. He had spent well over three months sleeping on the ground, and the mattress felt alien to him. The thin bedspread smelled of tobacco and God knew what else, but the smells didn't bother Slocum. His own unwashed body was overpowering enough, reeking of sour sweat and the musty scent of wet horsehair. The soft mattress engulfed him and he drifted into a sound sleep.

He dreamed of wild cows, their hides covered with strange brands. He dreamed of horses and gunfire, and the faces of dead men drifted like clouds before him, appearing and disappearing at random. He saw the faces of women, too, but they were shadowy and elusive, like images in a running stream. He heard the knock of a woodpecker on a hollow hickory tree, and the thud of footsteps somewhere beyond his vision, disembodied, but oddly threatening.

Something, a sound perhaps, jolted him out of the dream. He drifted up through layers of sleep, straining to hear, trying to define the faint noise. No, it wasn't a sound, it was more of a *feeling* that reached Slocum's nerves and sounded an alarm. He sat up quickly, listening. He heard nothing but silence, and yet the silence was alive. It breathed, and its breathing told Slocum danger lurked. But where? Outside his window? In the hall?

Slocum picked up his saddlebags, gripping the straps like the handle of a club, and peered through the window.

It was mid-evening, judging from the size of the crowds. The same tinny music, the same raucous, off-key laughter as at Dodge drifted to his ears, but he saw no danger. There were no shadowy figures standing on porches watching his window, no man approached the hotel with his pistol's hammer-thong unlatched.

The danger must lie in the hallway outside his room.

Slocum thought about it. The only way he could escape through the window was to jump ten feet to the ground, because his room was on the second story. If a man jumped ten feet, he might get away. On the other hand, he might break a leg—look what had happened to Booth when he shot Lincoln.

The only way out was through the door, and the only way to do that was fast. He could take whoever waited by surprise. He had to act first, because whoever waited was likely about to commit the same strategy himself. He would either sneak the door, which was unlocked, open, or he would break in, fire at the figure on the bed, and disappear.

Slocum tensed. He drew his Colt quietly, steeled himself, then flung the door open. Two men were there. One was the young cowboy Slocum had overpowered back at the herd. Without a word, Slocum swung the barrel of his pistol down on the head of the young cowboy. Then he crashed the barrel down on the crown of the cowboy's companion. Slocum wanted no shots fired. He could have killed them both, but he was not a killer by nature. If there was any other way, he would take it, and this was the way. The second fellow hadn't been knocked unconscious by the blow, so Slocum gave him a second lick. The man lay still, and Slocum raced down the hall—but light-footed, so as not to attract attention.

He passed through the lobby, and after he felt it was safe in the street, ran to the stable. He saddled Wind, made sure his bedroll and saddlebags were in place, then left. He turned toward Dodge. He had business in Dodge, business with Earl Blake and whoever else—and Slocum was certain there *was* somebody else—was involved. That tall man he had seen through the window of the general store, maybe.

As he found the trail, he groaned. He was bone-weary. He seemed to have been forever on the run. When would he find a good bed in which he could sleep all night without people sneaking up on him?

So much to do, and so little time. He was going to have to see Ken Dorsey's sister in Dodge. He didn't like to bring bad news to anybody, but he was duty-bound not only to tell Marisa about how Ken had met his death, but to give her Ken's wages, too. He would do that first, before he looked up Earl Blake. Maybe he could bluff his way into getting Blake to admit something. It was a chance he was going to take. Three of his men needed avenging.

7

Marisa Dorsey was furious. She was angry from the tip of her pert nose to her fists, which she kept clenching and unclenching. She paced the floor restlessly, wishing with all her heart that she was a man. If she were a man, she could saddle a horse and hunt that killer, John Slocum, down. When she found him, she would shoot him dead. He deserved worse, but that was all she could think of in her blind rage. She would blow his brains away with the .44 her brother had taught her to shoot.

Marisa had been ill with a cold. She was not accepting business in her home shop. She did not subscribe to the *Globe*, because a seamstress did not make enough money to waste it on newspapers. Ken had told her to use what she wanted from the money he left with her, but she refused to spend a dime. That money was his, and she put it in the bank so that his dream of a ranch of his own would one day come true.

The news of her brother's death had reached her second-hand, five days old. She met a friend shopping downtown, after her cold cleared up, and the friend had sympathized. *Sympathized!* My God, it was like a knife in her side.

Her brother had been killed by rustlers, and it was said that John Slocum, the trail boss, had been in cahoots with the thieves. It was said he had killed Ned Blake outright, and was the cause of Ken's death.

She had gone to Earl Blake at once. Blake assured her that what she had heard was true. The trusted trail boss, his honored partner, had turned bad. Why he himself had lost not only his brother, but at least twenty-five thousand dollars worth of beef. Marisa was somewhat comforted when Blake said that a posse had been searching for Slocum. When he was found, he would be treated as all cow thieves were treated. Blake didn't finish the sentence. There was no need to. Marisa knew the ways of the West. Those who committed a crime against society were punished according to the crime. Horse thieves and cattle rustlers were hanged.

But she didn't want John Slocum to hang. She wanted to finish him herself. Oh, if she were a man! She'd get a horse and roam the plains until she found the cowardly beast.

For a day, Marisa toyed with the idea of doing as she wished, anyway. The devil take custom. Custom dictated that a woman didn't hunt for rustlers, even if they killed her brother. That was man's work. But, so far, the men had come back with nothing. *She* could do better. She could ride, she knew how to follow a trail, she knew how to shoot better than many men. Why shouldn't she become a one-woman posse, a sort of avenging angel?

The more she thought about it, the better she liked the idea, but there was one hitch: She didn't own a horse. She would have to buy one, or borrow one from a friend. Questions would be asked—why this sudden interest in a horse? Shouldn't she be in mourning for Ken? Shouldn't she visit his grave? If she were to go anywhere, shouldn't she recover his body and bring it to Dodge for a decent burial?

Blake's men had brought Ned in. It could be done.

Damn John Slocum!

As she paced the floor, Marisa's frustration, anger, and grief reached such a point that she stopped pacing long enough to drag the .44 out of her dresser drawer. It was a Colt Army percussion weapon, worn, but still in good shape.

A knock sounded on the door. Marisa quickly hid the pistol under the sofa, straightened out her dress with a brush of her hands, and opened up.

A tall man looked down at her. It was night, and the only light was from the yellow rays of her kerosene lamp, but even in that dim light she could see that the man's eyes were green, and his hair black as night. He stood quietly, hat in hand, gazing at her, and in his eyes Marisa saw the hunger she often saw in men's eyes. She fought the blush, but it crept into her cheeks in spite of her effort. To make up for what she considered an unladylike display, she spoke more brusquely than she intended.

"What do you want?"

"I'd like to come in," he replied, in a strong but hushed voice. "I have something for you, Marisa."

The girl stepped back in surprise. She hadn't expected to hear her name. "Do I know you?" she asked.

"No, but I know you through your brother, Ken."

"Ken! Where did you know . . . ?"

Marisa paused. Sudden intuition told her exactly who it was who stood in her doorway. This had to be John Slocum. Her fury returned, but now it was mingled with shock and puzzlement. The man had nerve, she thought. Now that she was face to face with the man she believed to be her brother's killer, she was not so sure of herself. Instead, she felt a strange fascination for this tall, rugged man who was apparently, according to Blake and others, a cattle thief and a murderer. Would she, she wondered, have the nerve to kill him here in her own home? Could she take the life of a man so vital, so alive, in cold blood? She fought down a cold shudder, and forced a smile.

"Come in," she said in as normal a voice as possible.

Slocum stepped inside and quickly closed the door behind him. Marisa did not latch it, but stepped away from him as if she were afraid. He thought her behavior curious, but he put it down to her grief. Surely someone must have told her about Ken by now.

"Sit down," said Marisa coolly.

Slocum sat in a chair opposite the sofa. Marisa sat on the cushion above where the .44 lay hidden. She could reach it in a split second, if it came to that.

"What do you have for me?" she asked, marveling at the even quality of her voice. Her anger was like a volcano pressing just under the surface, ready to explode.

Slocum dug into his pocket and laid some money on the sofa beside Marisa. "These are Ken's wages," he said. "That and his bonus."

Marisa's anger could no longer submit to suppression. "You mean to tell me that you have the gall to bring me his wages, after what you did to him?"

She reached under the sofa and pulled out the .44. She cocked the trigger and pointed it at Slocum's chest. Her action caught Slocum by surprise. He stared at her, slack-jawed, the faint light from the oil lamps flickering in his green eyes.

"I'm going to shoot you dead, John Slocum," she said evenly. The hand holding the .44 did not waver.

Startled, Slocum stared at the black muzzle of the pistol. "Hey," he objected, "what is this?"

"You killed my brother," said the girl, "and Ned Blake. Now I'm going to kill you."

Slocum knew that he was in one of the most dangerous situations of his life. A squeeze of Marisa's finger and he'd be dead. At this range, she could scarcely miss. And the woman was dead serious.

"I never killed your brother," Slocum said evenly. "I never killed Ned, for that matter."

"Earl Blake says you did."

"Is the word of Earl Blake gospel around here?"

"He's a powerful man, and his word means a lot."

"He was my partner, and he's a crook. He's turned this whole sorry mess around to make it look like I was the bad man."

"He's succeeded. Dodge is against you, and Blake has posted a two-thousand-dollar reward for you, dead or alive."

Slocum whistled. "It was a thousand at first. Price is going up. I haven't been worth that much for a long time." He eyed the unwavering .44. "And you'd like to cash in on the reward?"

"That's an insult, Mister. I want *you*."

Her anger made her nostrils flare, and now he saw the clean lines of her face, the straight nose, the full lips. Ken had told him they were half Spanish and half Irish, and the best of both races showed up in the Dorseys. Marisa had flame-rust auburn hair. Her eyes were a startling blue. She had a lovely figure. It was a hell of a thing to be thinking at a time like this, but the woman was a beauty, and if she wasn't about to blow out his heart, he might have given her a compliment. The flash of her eyes warned him that each word he spoke from now on was important—if he was to stay alive.

"I wish you'd let me explain my side of it," he said softly. "I liked your brother. I think he liked me some, too. You get to know a man on a long drive like that. He was a man to ride the river with. I'm sorry as hell he got killed. But I didn't do it, lady, and if you pull that trigger, you'll be making one hell of a mistake."

Marisa's trigger finger tightened. Slocum tensed. Marisa's brows wrinkled in a frown. Slocum sucked in a quick breath, held it. If she so much as sneezed, that damned pistol would go off.

For the first time Marisa's resolve wavered. Her hand began to tremble slightly. The barrel of the pistol moved slightly off-center. There was something wrong here. Would this tall, handsome man who should never have been in Dodge at all, but somewhere on the trail to safety, risk his life to see her, to bring her Ken's pay, if he had done what they all said he did?

Taking advantage of Marisa's indecision, Slocum said quickly, "Look, I know it seems bad. Blake said I was responsible for the rustling. He put a two-thousand-dollar reward on my head. He has convinced the law that I'm guilty, as well as the people of Dodge, but listen: I know who is guilty."

"Who?" Marisa's pistol never wavered. She feared a trick, a diversion to put her off guard.

"Earl Blake."

"You're crazy! He's well thought of in Dodge."

"How long has he been here?"

"Well, I don't know, really."

"From about the time the rustling got worse?"

Slocum was shooting in the dark now. He had no idea if there had ever been such a dividing line, but he hoped to play on Marisa's imagination.

The girl frowned. "I honestly don't know," she admitted. "I haven't paid that much attention, but it does seem like I've heard Ken say the rustling had increased over the past year."

"About the time Blake arrived?"

The pistol veered a little more off-center. "Well, I'm not sure, but maybe. Yes."

Slocum pursued his advantage.

"Would I take the trouble to bring you Ken's wages if I were guilty? Hell, girl, I'd be on the trail for parts south, and you know it."

"I've thought of that."

She touched the coins Slocum had laid by her side. She picked one up and put it to her cheek. There were tears in her dark eyes.

"He wanted his own ranch so much!"

"He'd have been good at it, too."

"Yes. Ken was good at anything he tried."

"Did you know he was my assistant on the drive, and that I demoted Ned Blake to give him the job?"

Marisa's eyes flashed fire. "Then it was Ned who killed him. He did it out of spite and jealousy."

Slocum shook his head. "No, I don't think so. Ned had bigger fish to fry. He was the inside man for his brother, and I have no doubt Ned's percentage would have been plenty."

"How do you know this?"

"I don't have positive proof, but I do know what happened to the cattle."

Slocum told the girl about his trip to Ellsworth. He told her about finding the Pollywog cows, and how the brands had been changed to the Rolling Log. He told her of his meeting with Blake and about Ord Wade who had stopped him on the trail that first day. He and Blake were thick. Slocum was convinced that the two had had much to do with the rustling and the killings, and the reason that he had not gone south was that he wanted to avenge the deaths of Ken and his two other friends, Bobby and Tubs. He was determined to find the rustlers and bring them to justice. He would also be clearing his own name in the process. His name, he said, was important to him. He was a Georgia man, and in Georgia a man's honor was held high.

Slocum spoke convincingly, and Marisa found herself, reluctantly at first, believing the man she had planned to kill. "That Ord Wade," she said suddenly. "I know him."

"Oh?"

Slocum was surprised.

"He's been coming around. I think he'd like to keep company with me."

"For once, I'll have to give that fellow credit. He has good taste."

Marisa felt her color rise. She was flustered, and she didn't like it. Her lips stiffened, and she raised her pistol

again, but Slocum reached over and took it from her. She
didn't resist. Then he handed it back to her, butt first.

"If you want to shoot," he told her, "now is the time."

She laid the pistol aside.

"I don't know what to think," she said huskily. "I hated
you when you came through that door, but . . ."

"You don't now?"

"No," she said softly. "I don't now." All of a sudden,
she crumpled up and began to sob. Her shoulders shook
and her hair fell over her face.

Slocum moved to her side. He took her in his arms and
held her. She made no move to resist, but leaned against
him, resting her thick auburn hair on his shoulder. The feel
of it was sensuous, and he realized he had been a long time
without a woman. He stroked the long, silky strands, and
talked softly to Marisa.

"I think," he said, "we are on the same side."

"Yes. Oh, I don't know! I don't know what to think."

Slocum continued to stroke her hair, and the girl shivered as the tips of his fingers caressed her back. But she
didn't draw away. He dabbed at the tears flowing down her
face, ran a finger under her eyes. Her sobs diminished as
he patted her gently on the back, rubbed the back of her
shoulders.

Slocum felt a warmth in his loins, and he sensed similar
emotions were slipping up on Marisa. She looked up at
him and he kissed her red, full lips. She responded by
returning his kiss with a hunger as deep as his own.

"My God," she murmured, "what are we doing? I
hardly know you."

"We know each other well enough," he replied. "We
know what we need and what we want from each other.
Even though we have known each other for only a short
time, does it matter? I feel as if I've known you forever,
Marisa. Ken talked about you so much. And maybe something inside you knows me, too."

He kissed her again, and she responded without reservation. Her tongue sought the corners of his mouth, and her hand slipped down between his thighs.

"Here," she whispered, "wait."

She pulled away and undressed completely. Yards and yards of dress, petticoats, and underdrawers slid to the floor in seconds, and she lay in his arms again.

"Get undressed," she murmured. Slocum peeled out of his clothes and stood before her naked, his body glistening with sweat, golden in the lampglow.

"Now," she murmured.

Slocum kissed her as he lay her down on the divan, covered her with his body, then tongued each dark, hard nipple. He worked his warm, moist tongue down the length of Marisa's naked body.

Slocum rolled her over on her back and spread her legs apart. Then he slipped his pulsing organ in between the hot lips. In and out, down and up, in and out, down and up. He felt the tension building, and there would be no stopping.

They came together with a great cry, and she ground her hips against him, driving hard to retain him, to hold the pressure of him.

It had been a long, long time, and he wasn't about to stop. Marisa's heat again mounted, and she surged up against him. She rolled him over on his back, and they pumped together until they came once again. Only this time they didn't cry out. Their lips were locked in a fierce embrace as they both burned with the sensation.

After the second time, Slocum gazed up into Marisa's blue eyes. Her face was framed in the auburn hair, and her nipples rested soft and pliant against his chest.

"Do you still hate me?" he asked.

She touched his lips with hers. "I needed that as much as you did," she answered. "No, I'll never hate you again. Not ever."

"Do you believe me?"

"Yes, John Slocum," she whispered, "I believe you."

She did things to him then that made him want her again.

And to hell with everything else. For now, there was only Marisa and the sweet depths of her, the warmth of her arms around his sweat-soaked bare back, the soft touch of her lips on his loins.

"You're the strongest man I've ever known," she sighed, when he had finished again. "But don't you think it's time I took you to my bed?"

Slocum laughed harshly as she reached for the lamp by the divan, and turned the wick down low.

"I never turn down a fair offer," he rasped.

8

Slocum felt good. It was the best he'd felt in months, perhaps years. Marisa Dorsey was a good lover. Her response to him had been what he needed, both physically and mentally. The pale light of morning made the simple room stand out starkly from the lingering shadows of night.

He stretched mightily, his whole body tightening from arms to toes in one great stretch of pleasure.

Marisa's eyes opened and she smiled up at him. Her hair was askew, the limp auburn tresses spreading over her pillow like a fan.

"You feel good now, don't you?" she asked.

"Yes. I feel wonderful."

"Was I all right?"

"You know the answer to that, Marisa. I don't have to tell you. Where does the passion come from, the Spanish side or the Irish?"

"Don't you think the combination doubles the heat?"

He kissed her, and glanced down at her breasts resting

on his chest. They were as clean as if a cat had licked them, while he smelled like the downstream waters of the Brazos after five thousand head of longhorns had churned the waters black.

"Good God," he whispered, "you've made love to a man who hasn't had a bath in months."

"Do you think I paid any attention to that?"

"No, but I want to get clean. How about a good hot tub before breakfast?"

"I'll draw us both a bath," she said lightly, "and I'll fix my man the best breakfast he ever ate."

Marisa left him, and as she dressed—slipping into her dress only, and leaving the undergarments—he admired her firm body. Slocum had had many women. To him, they had all been beautiful, and he never compared, but if Marisa wasn't the most lovely, she was unique. The passion in her was unique. Who would have thought this quiet, beautiful seamstress would have known so much about making love to a man? Still waters ran deep.

She put kettles and buckets of water on the kitchen range, and stoked the fire. In the meantime, Slocum took a chance. He left by the back door and saw to Wind, tethered to Marisa's back fence. He had left Wind saddled, not knowing just what to expect. He set the saddle aside and patted his faithful spotted horse.

"There's grass in this yard," he whispered, "but I'll see if I can rustle you some oats."

He returned to the house. "Do you have any oats?" he asked. "Wind could use some."

"Wind? That your horse?"

"Yeah."

"Oh." Marisa looked at him, her eyes alive with mischief. "No, I don't have any oats. People who don't own horses usually don't have oats. Shall I go next door and borrow a cup?"

She seized a mug and pretended to head for the door. "I'm sure I can borrow a cup," she began, but Slocum snatched her to him and gave her a kiss on her full lips.

"That will be enough of that," he said, grinning. "*I'll* find oats someplace."

"What are you planning?" Marisa was no longer joking. Her eyes were clouded with apprehension.

"Wind needs oats," Slocum told her. "You got a pail, at least? I'll fetch him some from the livery."

"Be careful," she said, as he left by the back door, on foot.

"I'll be right back," he said, and it was damned hard to tear himself away from her.

He kept to the sunless side of the house and made his way to the livery stable. It was quiet on the streets, and he saw no one. The stable, too, was untended. He found a fifty-pound sack of oats and filled the pail to the brim. He made it back to the house without being seen. He fed and watered Wind, then tied him in the sheltered shadows of Marisa's rear porch. It would never do for Wind to wander the yard. Unwanted eyes would look closer, since it would be known Marisa had no horse, and Slocum owned one of the few spotted saddle carriers in the country. It would be a simple matter of putting two and two together, and Slocum wasn't ready for that. He hadn't finished putting one and one together. He wanted more of Marisa Dorsey. Much more.

He was about to enter the house when he heard a male voice. He recognized it instantly as Ord Wade's.

"I saw your smoke from your chimney, and thought I'd see why you was up so early," he was saying.

"That's nice of you, Mr. Wade, but I was only taking a bath."

"It's pretty early in the day for a bath, isn't it?"

"Is that any of your business, Mr. Wade?"

"Well, now, don't get huffy with me, miss. I don't like it."

"What does it take to let you know I'm not interested, Mr. Wade?"

"Drop the 'Mr. Wade,' will you? To my friends, I'm Ord."

"I'm no friend of yours, and I never will be."

Ord's voice growled in anger.

"Why not? What's the matter with me? I'm a successful businessman in town, Marisa. You could do worse. I've got good connections with Earl Blake and Lew Ponca. I'm going places."

"Only because you can use those, Mr. Wade."

"These sixguns? Naw! I wear them just to impress people. They don't mean anything."

"That's not what I heard."

"Gossip is cheap."

"Will you leave, please?"

"Aw, Marisa, come on. Just a little kiss, and then I'll go. Give me a little encouragement for a change, so's I'll know I'm on the right track with you."

"The only track you'll be right on is the one out the door."

Slocum nodded with approval. The girl had spunk.

"Come on!" Ord Wade's voice was husky, urgent. "Come on, just one kiss."

"Get away. I'll holler for help if you don't."

"Marisa, please." The voice was pleading. Suddenly, the voice changed to a bellow of pain and outrage, accompanied by the sounds of splashing water.

"God damn it, woman! Why'd you do that?"

"To show you I mean business."

"God damn it," the voice raged on, "all over my gun hand, too. Hell, I'll be crippled for a week."

"Get out of here."

There was a silence, and Slocum tensed. Silence of this sort meant trouble. One cry from Marisa and he would barge through the door.

But apparently Ord Wade had reconsidered.

"I'll get you," Slocum heard him say. "I want you, and I'll get you."

"Get out," said Marisa coldly.

There was the sound of booted feet stamping across the floor, and a door slammed. Slocum waited a few moments, then entered. Marisa glanced at him, her face flushed.

"Did you hear him?" she asked.

"I heard."

"The bastard!"

"That he is."

"Well, I got him good." The girl smiled wickedly. "I meant to scald him you know where, but he covered up with his hand."

"His gun hand, poor fellow."

"Yes."

Slocum kissed her willing lips and held the girl close.

"God," she said, "I was afraid you'd come in any moment."

"If he had tried anything more serious than talk, I would have."

She kissed him. Slocum felt his excitement rise, and he guided her hand to him. She grasped him through the protective covering of his trousers. Then she stopped and unbuttoned his trousers.

"Do you like this?" she asked as she fondled him. Slocum nodded, too dazed with pleasurable sensation to speak. He was gripping the top of a counter so hard that his knuckles were white.

They took a bath together in a long galvanized tub that Marisa brought out of a storage closet. She washed him, and he washed her, taking care that he explored every opening, mount, and mound thoroughly. When they were finished, Marisa was so excited that she led him to the sofa, where they made love again.

"You must think me shameless," she said, when he climbed from her body.

"No more'n me." He grinned.

"It—it's just that I've never met a man like you.

Heavens, I just look at you and get all excited." She sat up and rubbed her palm over the muscles in his arm. Slocum could feel her heat and the tug at his loins. But he knew there was nothing left for her, not for at least a little while.

"You said something about fixing breakfast," he ventured.

"Yes, maybe that will take my mind off . . ."

She laughed, sprang to her feet, then danced away like a merry nymph. Slocum watched her go and let out a longing sigh. She looked good with or without clothes, and she had given him all she had—and more. "Some woman," he muttered to himself before he padded across the floor. He felt good, keen as a knife edge, strong.

Marisa fixed steak and eggs, fried potatoes, and slabs of bread, all washed down with coffee the way he liked it, black and hot.

As they ate, she talked.

"We know that Blake and Wade are your enemies," she said, "and I think there is somebody else."

"Is he a tall fellow, good dresser, gray-haired, mean face?"

Marisa was surprised. "That's him. How did you know Lew Ponca?"

Slocum told her about his experience when he broke into the general store.

The girl nodded. "I think those three are in something together, but I don't know what."

"What makes you suspicious?"

"The first time Ponca rode into Dodge, he came with Ned Blake."

So there was Ned's tie to the group.

"And that was about a year ago?" he asked.

Marisa nodded.

"You don't see much of Ponca," she said, "but he has the money, I think. Blake is his representative in Dodge."

"And other places?"

"Yes, and Ord Wade works for him, not Blake."

"You know a lot about what goes on around here."

"I get a lot of gossip in my business—and of course there's Wade."

"Does he talk?"

"When I give him the chance."

Slocum felt the smallest nip of jealousy. "That's all he gets, I hope," he retorted, "a chance to talk."

Marisa drew back her hand and slapped him hard across the face. The blow made a sharp report in the kitchen. It left red marks streaked across his tanned face.

Slocum, his temper flashing, slapped Marisa back. Welts to match his raised on her lovely face, and she tore into him. She struck and pounded with her clenched fists.

"Damn you!" she raged. "This is what I should have done in the first place!"

As she fought him, Slocum's own temper dissolved. He was ashamed of his jealousy and his remark. He avoided her flying fists, and finally pinned her arms down to her side. Then he kissed her hard. She struggled briefly, then stopped, and returned his kiss with a vengeance.

Slocum drew back.

"You are," he said, "the goddamnedest woman I've ever known."

"You're a puzzle yourself," said the girl, but she smiled. "I have the feeling there's still a lot of heat in both of us, and I can think of better ways to use it up than by fighting. Come along."

She took him by the hand and led him from the kitchen.

"Where are we going?" Slocum asked.

"To bed. If you think it was good on the sofa, you don't know the half of it yet."

9

Llewellyn Ponca, who liked to be called Lew by his associates and friends, warmed to the juices of success. They flowed through his body like honeyed butter. He was in an expansive mood.

"Whiskey for my friends," he called to the bartender.

His friends, ringed around the table with him, were Earl Blake, Ord Wade, and a young man named Lucius Carp, who had two Colts slung low on his hips.

They were in Varieties, a saloon that was a favorite meeting place for Lew Ponca. More business deals had been formed over a friendly glass in Varieties than in any stuffy office, so far as he was concerned. In fact, Lew Ponca had no office. He often bragged that his office was in his hip pocket. No matter where he went to make his deals, whether land speculation or cattle, his office was with him.

"That way," he said, "there are no delays. When a deal is ready, close it. None of that 'Come to the office at nine tomorrow' stuff for me. A deal could turn cold by then. Yes, strike while the iron is hot, I say."

Ponca thought of himself as an entrepreneur. He dealt in land and cattle—a dangerous combination since land-owners resented the free-riding cattlemen, and the cattle-men resented the tight-lipped, wire-fencing landowners. And Ponca was also a lobbyist for the railroad interests, both in the state of Kansas and in Washington, D.C. As a lobbyist he had been very successful in procuring land for the Kansas Pacific Railroad. At least in part because of his efforts, the KP was able to push on to Hays and points west.

Accepting money for his efforts had been only part of Ponca's deal with the KP. He also asked for, and received, a lower rate for shipping his cattle. When cattle were shipped by the thousands, the dollars in difference were enriching, to say the least. And when the cattle were free, the profits were enormous.

The fact that the cattle were practically free, gathered at a cost of mere wages, was a well-kept secret between Ponca and Earl Blake. Ord Wade knew, too, and Ord also knew who the real boss was, but aside from him and Blake, none of the men who did the dirty work knew. They knew Blake and Wade. It was enough; they didn't care. All they cared about was their cut. Money earned loyalty and closed mouths. Without the money, they'd be gone, to a man.

Kansas Pacific had no idea that the cattle Ponca deliv-ered to them via Blake were rustled. They did know that their business increased because of the arrangement, and they were happy about that. The Santa Fe was a big outfit and could run them out of business with its longer tracks, better rolling stock, and solid financial backing. The KP welcomed Ponca's cattle. If necessary, they would have dropped the shipping price still more and still made money, but they didn't tell Ponca that.

People had no idea that Ponca was crooked. He was

well-liked wherever he went. He openly admitted his lob-
bying activities, and in Ellsworth he was looked upon as
something of a hero, because of his success. On the other
hand, Earl Blake was looked upon as a great benefactor
because of the large herds he brought to the Ellsworth
loading pens. Nobody questioned his not taking the cattle
to Dodge. Blake explained that he preferred the Kansas
Pacific's handling of his cattle over the treatment given
them by Santa Fe, and that satisfied everybody who was
involved on the receiving end. Business was booming. Lit-
erally hundreds of thousands of beeves were being shipped
east every year. Dodge was getting the lion's share of this
bonanza, so nobody thought very much of what Blake did
with his.

Lew Ponca had arrived in Dodge the year before with
Ned Blake. Prior to his arrival, Ponca's only occupation
had been that of lobbyist for the KP. After he had success-
fully completed his mission for the railroad, he decided to
travel west to see what the country looked like. He immediately ingratiated himself with the powers in the Kansas
capital. Step number one in his lexicon of success was to
know where the money lay. There was no better place to
learn about this than in the capitals of the United States,
even Topeka.

He quickly learned that there were two enterprises in
Kansas that made money: selling land to settlers and cattle
dealing. He had already thought about cattle, hence his
arrangement with Kansas Pacific. What he hadn't thought
about was free cattle. A young puncher named Ned Blake
had become his mentor in the matter of cattle. Ned knew
where to buy them, what to look for, what drives were, and
how to go about organizing them——or so he said. He also
knew about free cattle, what people in the country called
rustled cattle.

Lew Ponca was a capable man. His enterprises turned to
successful enterprises. Ever since he was a boy in Pennsyl-
vania and had hawked sandwiches at carriage stops, he had

always made money. And he quickly learned that he made more money by using cheaper grades of meat but charging top prices for his sandwiches. He learned early on that stretching the truth in commercial matters quite often netted great profit.

Another thing about Ponca was his greed. He made no secret about this to himself. He wanted money, and a great deal of it. He would get money by fair means or foul, because money meant power. And Lew Ponca wanted power. The need for power was ingrained in him. After a year in Kansas, he was becoming that power. Legislators in Topeka came to him for money when they were in need. Cattlemen gave him deals because he paid in cash. Homesteaders went to him for land, because he had purchased many of the choice areas. When his young friend Ned Blake mentioned ways to get more money quickly, he listened.

Though Ellsworth had much going for it, and was Ponca's shipping point for his cattle, Dodge City was the most active of the cowtowns. The most deals, crooked or otherwise, were made in Dodge, and Ponca spent much of his time at the Dodge House.

During his first month in Dodge, he played the game of buying and selling cattle honestly. In the meantime, Ned had introduced him to his brother, Earl. Ponca watched Earl Blake. The man had been a drifter before he arrived in Dodge, but he was now a successful gambler. Sometimes he was accused of whipping an ace off the bottom of the deck for himself, and when that happened, Earl Blake was quick to break the head of the accuser. Ponca liked that. He trusted men who were like himself. He didn't know if Blake cheated at cards. Chances were he did. Ned, Earl's brother, was interested in rustling cattle; wouldn't the thread of dishonesty run in the family? Ponca decided it would. Blake was a bluff, hearty fellow whom most people tolerated. When he spoke of cattle prices, people listened, because he had a sixth sense regarding the market.

After his first month in Dodge, Ponca took Blake into his confidence. At first he pretended mere inquisitiveness. He asked seemingly innocent questions about rustling. Blake had the answers. As the acquaintanceship deepened, the intimacy between the two men ripened to a point where Ponca felt he could trust Blake. Ponca finally told Blake what was on his mind.

"I figured that," Blake said.

"Was I that obvious?"

"Listen, a man with your money and background doesn't waste time on idle jawing. When you started in on free beef, I figured there was more to it."

"Well, what about it? I will give you a cut of any herds you can deliver to the Kansas Pacific in Ellsworth."

"I think," said Blake, "we can come to terms."

As it turned out, Blake was not a newcomer to the rustling game. He had turned several herds of private origin into free beef. They weren't large herds, and had served as practice runs for larger gains. He had used various drovers, none of them suspecting that dishonest work was afoot. With Ned as his accomplice on the trail drives, he had stolen the cattle away each time at a crucial point along the trail. Sometimes the drover had been deliberately shot, just in case he had suspected something. On this last enterprise, when John Slocum had been his "partner," Blake had put the word out that Slocum must be killed. In the confusion, his brother had died instead, and one of his men had been wounded.

Blake blamed Slocum for Ned's death. He made certain that people of Dodge as well as the marshal's office believed it, too. He also posted a two-thousand-dollar reward to back his statements. Yet, in the center of his mind, where he kept intimate thoughts like valuable papers in a vault, he entertained doubt. Was it just possible that Ponca had given orders? Had Ned known too much? Earl Blake knew well enough the axiom of the outlaw order: Too many tongues could hang the chief. Blake didn't doubt for a moment that Ponca had his own spy on the drive. He could have been one of the regular crew or, more likely, an itinerant cowboy who worked for a week or so, then drew his pay. Blake knew about Ned's being replaced on the drive by Ken Dorsey. Had Ned shown any resentment? If so, Ponca might have lost trust in him.

Things were not as straightforward as they seemed. In this, even the bull-necked, hearty Earl Blake recognized an irony. Crooks had problems with their help as well as any honest man.

Irony. Like now. Here they were, all sitting at a table in Varieties, drinking together, pretending to be great friends. Ponca was speaking. Blake, who liked good clothes, allowed himself a twinge of envy concerning his associate's clothing. Ponca liked gray coloring, in accord with his graying hair, as he pointed out, laughing. His suits fit perfectly, and his boots were handmade and of supreme quality. Since coming west, Lew Ponca had affected the boots as a method of fitting right in. A man of the West wore the best boots he could afford. People were apt to look at a man's boots before they took a good look at his face. They symbolized a man's status and his feelings about the country in which he lived. They told of his occupation, the different shapes and heels revealing if the owner was a cowboy, a bartender, a businessman, a trapper, or a homesteader. Ponca's boots told the world he was rich, and that was all the world of Dodge City needed to know.

They were speaking in low tones.

"I like the way things went," said Ponca. "The arrangement will make us all a nice bit of change."

"It went fine, except for Ned," said Blake. He was fishing for reactions, and watched the faces of Ponca and Wade closely.

Neither revealed anything except sorrow.

"He was a good friend," said Ponca, reaching over to pat Blake's hand. "I can't tell you how sorry I am."

"Yeah," said Wade, "I liked him, too."

Blake withdrew his hand from Ponca's touch, slightly embarrassed by the other man's show of emotion. Blake was pleased, however, if a bit puzzled. Ponca had never before shown any emotion over the killing that had taken place during their operations. His eye was on the bottom line of the balance sheet. That was all that counted.

"Well," said Blake, "here's to my brother. May he rest in peace."

The four men drank to that.

"And damn John Slocum," Blake went on loudly, so all could hear. "He caused my brother's death. He rustled those Pollywog cattle. He is a thief and a killer, and my offer of two thousand in cash for that bastard, dead or alive, stands."

There were murmurs of agreement in the saloon. Men checked their pistols and thought of rifles. "Dead or alive," Blake had said. John Slocum was a dangerous man, and many in the room knew it. But two thousand dollars in cash was more than the ordinary trail driver made in five years. It was a goal worth going for, even if a little bushwhacking were in order.

Ponca ordered another drink. "Leave the bottle," he told the bartender. "Ned Blake was my friend. We need a drink or two." He raised his voice. "Hear me?" he called to the room. "Ned Blake was my friend, and I'll add a thousand to the two Earl has offered."

There was an audible gasp from the onlookers. Three thousand!

John Slocum was a dead man.

Into this circle of excitement pounced a young cowboy. He crashed through the swinging doors of Varieties like a bowlegged whirlwind, and stomped over to the mourner's table.

He addressed both Ponca and Blake at the same time, since they were sitting side by side.

"You thieves!" he shouted. "You killers! You're the ones who have been doing the rustling around here!"

The room grew very quiet. Death stalked among the tables and chairs.

"Why do you say that?" asked Ponca quietly.

"I've proof," said the cowboy with heat. "Damned good proof."

Ponca glanced ever so briefly at Wade, but the glance was loaded. It said: Kill him.

10

If Slocum enjoyed himself in bed with Marisa, he swore
that the girl got more out of it than he did. She was the
embodiment of carnal passion, and she gave him experiences such as he had never had before.

A couple of hours before midnight of his second night at
the girl's house, Slocum had had enough, and the girl slept
quietly beside him. He sat up and gazed at her smooth
face. Her auburn hair made a wavy frame around her fea-
tures, setting them off, enhancing them as a beautiful
frame will a lovely portrait.

He bent over and kissed the now pliant lips, cool and
accepting, but without response. Then he dressed quietly.
Remarks and character sketches given by Marisa at breakfast that morning began to surface. Ponca. Who was this
man Marisa suspected of pulling the strings?

As Slocum thought about Ponca, the urgency of the situation also surfaced. He had taken a recess from his troubles, but it was time to return to them, to clear his name,

and to avenge the death of good comrades.

Slocum was not a mild man by nature. He lived at the edge of disaster most of the time, and welcomed the challenges. When he was in danger, he felt most alive. Danger was food for his soul, and he welcomed it. There were times when that was noble, for he corrected wrongs by facing danger. There were times when it was foolish, because of the odds.

Right now he was about to commit a foolish act. He was going to find Ponca. He didn't know where Ponca was, but he was probably at the Varieties with Blake. He would try there first.

He dressed quickly, making sure that neither his belt buckle clinked nor his boots clomped. He didn't want to awaken Marisa. She would try to talk him out of his foolish errand, and he wouldn't be able to do so. That would anger her, and God knew what she would do then—throw something at him, maybe, or run out into the street screaming that the house was on fire. She might do anything to keep him from doing what he had to do.

He didn't kiss her again, for a kiss had its own magic; even the lightest brush of the lips would waken a sleeper. He had kissed her once and gotten away with it, but twice was chancy.

Slocum had no idea if he would return. If Ord Wade were present, along with any other gunmen that Ponca and Blake employed, he might not. He blew a kiss to the sleeping girl and left.

At the Varieties, the young cowboy, the accuser of Ponca and Blake, stood before the two men, his hands open at his sides, his legs apart. He was so mad, he didn't see Wade give a sign to Lucius Carp. He had made his statement, and he knew something was going to happen. He saw Ord Wade rise and disappear. Wade knew better than to get mixed up in a killing fight. Few men were as good as he when it came to sixgun duels. If he killed the cowboy, it would not be favored by the townsfolk, not even the tougher element. Fair play was almost like a law of the land, and if Wade made a killing it would not be considered fair play. He would let Carp do the job. Carp was unknown in these parts. He hailed from Abilene and other points. Wade, who kept his ear to the ground in such matters, knew that Carp was a killer, which was his main reason for putting him on the payroll. He would come in handy in situations just like this.

Another voice spoke up. It was the stentorian voice of Paul Meers, a well-known cattleman of the region.

"I think you're wrong, son," he said to the young cowboy, then looked at him closely. "Say, ain't you Caleb Fancher?"

"That I am," was the terse reply, "and I'm not wrong."

"Whoa, now," said Meers. "I happen to know that this Slocum feller ain't all lily-white. I heard he's got a reputation down South, and has served a little time. I'd consider that, Fancher."

But Fancher wasn't swayed.

"I got proof these two are the brains behind all the stealing," he declared, his face flushed red with anger. "Slocum? Well, I don't know about him. I *do* know about these two."

"I'm getting up a posse in the morning," Meers insisted. "I lost me sixty thousand dollars to a rustler—namely Slocum—and I aim to get either that money or his hide. Ponca and Blake are honest as the hills, young feller. Better back down and apologize."

"I don't apologize to anybody," said Fancher.

It was then that Lucius Carp began the process of doing what he was paid to do. He stood up and faced Fancher.

"You are talking bad about friends of mine," he said in a hard, dry voice. "I don't like it."

"It's none of your business," Fancher retorted. "Who're you? A damned ass licker?"

Carp flushed and walked a few paces off. Then he

turned and said, "You callin' me a ass licker, you son of a bitch?"

That was fighting talk. Everybody knew it, and the crowd, which had been pressed close, drew back. Even the bartender, who had seen many shootings and was bored with the whole thing, set down the glass he was wiping and went to the end of the bar.

Slocum entered at that moment. He saw in a single glance the positions of Blake and Ponca at the table. He saw Lucius Carp, a man he recognized as a frequenter of the owlhoot trail, and he saw Caleb Fancher. He knew right away that Fancher was not a gunfighter. His hand was poised like a claw over his sheathed sixgun. Before he dropped his hand two inches, Carp would put a bullet through his heart. Carp would let him start the draw first, of course. The courts called that self-defense.

"I'm calling you a damned ass licker," said Fancher. "So what are you going to do about it?"

The silence was intense as death waited to claim its victim. Fancher bent at the waist slightly, but Carp stood straight, calmly, coolly waiting, so he could earn his money.

Slocum barked, "Hold it!"

Eyes which had been riveted on Fancher and Carp swung to the speaker. There were exclamations of surprise. Here stood John Slocum, a man with a three-thousand-dollar price on his head, right in bullet range of the men who had made the offer. The man was a fool.

Fancher turned. "I can handle this," he said curtly. "Get out of the way."

Slocum advanced a few steps. "I'll take a hand in this game." He turned to Ponca and Blake. "You have two guns on this man, and he's not dry behind the ears yet. That's stacking it a little thick, wouldn't you say?"

"Slocum . . ." Blake started.

"Shut up," Slocum growled. "I do the talking from here on."

He paused a moment, waiting to see if Blake had anything to add. He didn't. Neither did Ponca, who was taking it all in with narrowed eyes.

Slocum drew his Colt. "Come out, Wade, or I'll shoot this coyote you got hired."

He pointed the pistol at Lucius Carp and cocked it.

Carp no longer looked so cool. His eyes shot sideways, and even his lips turned pale. He knew Slocum, just as Slocum knew him, from former times in other places, and he knew that Slocum was deadly.

In response to both Carp's wild look and Slocum's request, Wade stepped out from around a corner. Fancher gasped. He got the picture. If it so happened he killed Carp, Wade would shoot him, claiming to come to his friend's defense. It was a trap from which there was no escape. He retreated to Slocum's side.

"You draw your weapon and watch the rear," Slocum instructed him, and Fancher did so.

"You ain't goin' to get away with this, Slocum!" yelled Paul Meers. "I'm gettin' a posse together, and I'll track you straight into hell if I have to."

Slocum did not know Meers, and the man's anger interested him.

"What for?" he asked, keeping an eye on both Wade and Carp. "Who are you?"

"I'm Paul Meers, damn it. You ought to know; you stole enough of my cattle."

"I don't even know your brand," Slocum told him, and turned to Earl Blake. "I didn't kill Ned," he told Blake, "and I didn't rustle your cattle." He nodded at Lew Ponca. "If I was you I'd ask that man about Ned, and if I was the people around here, I'd ask you both about the herd."

He shoved the Colt back into its holster. On seeing that, Lucius Carp changed. The color returned to his face and his eyes lit up. Slocum was pleased.

"You talk big," Carp said to Slocum.

"I talk straight," said Slocum. "You are a coward and

you work for cowards. There is no honor in any of you."

Once again, these were fighting words, and the crowd drew back.

Carp smiled, and walked a few feet away once more.

"Say that again," he requested.

"Go to hell."

Carp's hand flashed. It was the last flash his hand ever made. His weapon was only halfway out of its holster when Slocum's Colt roared. The walls shivered and the overhead lights danced to the circling echoes. Lucius Carp spun over backward with a hole in the middle of his forehead.

Wade made a move, and Slocum shot into the floor at his feet.

"Don't try it," he warned. "I'd just as soon send you to Mr. Meers's hell as look at you. Put your hands in sight."

Wade raised his hands. He was furious. "I'll get you for this," he hissed.

"I'd like you to try." Slocum's voice was heavy with deadliness. He raised his Colt to Wade and cocked the hammer. A quick picture of his fake targeting of the three on the night he broke into the general store came back. There was no faking this time. He could take Wade and his partners, Blake and Ponca, right now, and save everybody a lot of trouble. He could, but he wouldn't. He couldn't even kill a man like Ord Wade in cold blood, and there had been enough killing for one night.

He let the hammer down easy.

"We'll meet again," he said, and turned to Fancher, who was keeping would-be reward seekers from becoming rich. "Let's go, and don't drop your gun barrel for the wink of an eye."

The two edged to the door.

Ponca licked dry lips. His hand started to move toward a concealed pistol. He saw Slocum's eyes on him, keen as a hawk's eyes, and stopped his movement. Slocum continued to stare at him in frank accusation until Ponca began to sweat. Finally the man in the gray suit averted his eyes.

Slocum's mouth twisted in a wry smile. He had the man sweating now. That was a start.

"First man out after us," said Slocum, "gets what he did." He pointed at Carp's body. Then he fired a shot into the ceiling. Everybody ducked, including Blake and Ponca. For all they knew, the bullet was meant for them.

Once outdoors, the two men ran for their horses. Slocum led the way down the main street of Dodge and into the darkness of the prairie. He glanced back and saw men fighting excited horses in an effort to climb aboard.

With the posse hot after them, they fled into the night. *Wind*, Slocum thought, *if you never win another race in your life, win this one.*

11

Dawn was shouldering black chunks out of the sky when the two men stopped. Their horses needed a break. Wind was sweating and the vapors spiralled upward from his flanks. Caleb Fancher's horse, a sorrel he called Whiskey, was in no better shape.

"Any sign?" Fancher asked in a whisper.

Slocum scanned the murky horizons. They were empty of hostile sight and sound. "We might have outrun them," he said cautiously.

Slocum didn't trust his own guesswork. In his experience, he had found that posses had a way of persistence. They might not be speedy, but they got there.

"I know a place where we can go," said Fancher.

"Where—and why in hell are you whispering?"

"I don't want to be heard."

"Who is going to hear you? And if they did, would it matter?"

"Naw." Fancher allowed a soft laugh. "I guess I'm just

nervous. I never had a posse after me before."

"Well, I haven't had that many myself, but there have been some experiences with them all right."

Caleb Fancher looked at his companion quizzically. "So you're John Slocum."

"That's right."

"I heard of you, and I guess Meers heard of you, too. You're not a Bat Masterson, but you're some kind of legend in these parts."

Slocum said nothing. The kid was beginning to rag at his nerves. They weren't out of it yet. He let the young cowhand stand there with egg on his face.

"All right, Slocum, I figure you're the one I've heard about. I got a right to know about the man who saved my hide."

"Have you?"

"How come you jumped into that fracas? It wasn't any of your concern."

"It was a lot of my concern, Fancher. Don't forget, I'm charged with rustling by the men you stood against."

"And Meers."

"And Meers. I don't like being called what I'm not."

"You aren't, then?"

"Aren't what?" Slocum prompted.

Caleb Fancher saw his error. "Hell," he muttered, "what do I know? Don't get riled if I ask dumb questions."

"You behaved like a fool tonight, and I pulled your hide out of the fire. Don't push your luck."

Fancher's own temper was not long on fuse. "Damn it," he snapped, "I said I made a mistake, didn't I? What do you want me to do—kiss your ass?"

Slocum grinned. He liked spunk, even if it was foolish spunk. "No. You can kiss Wind instead. He's an affectionate horse."

Fancher stared at Slocum hard for a moment. Then a slow grin spread across his face. "You're joshing me, aren't you?"

"We better get along, you and me. I have a hunch that posse's not far behind. We've got to find a place to hole up, make 'em all homesick." Slocum knew the ways of posses. Most of them were no better than mobs. Men who were only brave in a bunch, only fired up as long as the victim was outnumbered and not too hard to find. Once the going got rough, most of them would drop out. There were always one or two, however, who stuck like burrs to a sock. Those were the ones he was worried about: the cool-headed ones who went along for the hunt—and for the kill.

They both forgot words for a few seconds, listening. Slocum heard the ever-present Kansas wind; he heard a coyote howl and an early bird warble. He did not hear the clip of horses' hooves on the sun-hardened earth. He didn't hear the creak of saddle leather or the harsh, grunting mutters of men on posse duty.

That was good. Maybe he and Fancher had escaped. Maybe.

"They'll be bounty hunters," observed Fancher. "And they'll come alone. Those kind of people don't want to split their pot with anybody else."

With three thousand on his head, dead or alive, Slocum knew that Fancher's observation was all too true. There could be a dozen independent bounty hunters all looking for him. He was their great bonanza, their ticket to the good things in life, as long as the money lasted. And they, more than a posse, could become the real threats. They would shoot from ambush, and it would be a backshot. In spite of himself, Slocum shivered. He could almost feel the fatal ball as it smashed his spine.

"You're a cheerful bastard," Slocum growled to his young companion.

"Well, I'm just putting all the cards on the table."

"There's one hand you haven't called yet."

"What's that?"

"Where are we going to hide out?"

Fancher said, "I know a place."

"Lead on," said John Slocum. "The horses are all right now."

They weren't all right, as both men knew, but if a posse was out there somewhere, it didn't pay to linger.

Fancher led the way. They rode until the sun was high and hot. They watered their horses a couple of times in streams that meandered toward the Cimarron River. Always, they watched the back trail for signs of danger, but the plains remained empty of men on horseback.

The sun was getting to Slocum. He was tired. Not only had he killed a man, a distasteful matter for Slocum, even if the man had asked for it, but he'd made love at least half a dozen times with Marisa. He was still in trouble in Dodge, more than ever, and he still had to avenge the deaths of his three friends, Ken Dorsey, Tubs, and Bobby. He was tired, and impatient with the fact that he'd made no progress, except with Marisa. She had wanted to kill him; instead she had made love to him and left him exhausted.

"Damn it all," he growled to Caleb Fancher, "we been riding for hours. Are you sure you know where we're going?"

Fancher pointed to the southwest.

"My ranch, the Square U, lies in that direction. Before I got the ranch, I worked all over these parts as a cowhand. I know where I'm going."

True to his word, they arrived at a line cabin at high noon. It was a cottonwood log shack with a dirt floor. There was one dirty window in the west wall, and a plank door. In back there was a shed for the horses. A little stream bubbled nearby. The cabin and the shed were nestled in a grove of cottonwood trees, fairly well hidden from the casual eye.

"Pete Smith owns this place," said Fancher. "I used to work for him, but he doesn't run cattle any more. He's selling his property to settlers. Says he can make more money sitting on his butt than riding on it."

"Then we aren't apt to be interrupted by nosy line riders?"

"Nope."

"Thought we were going to your place."

"Hell," Fancher snorted. "The Square U is near a hundred miles from here. Three, four days of hard riding. Thought this'd be a better place to hole up for a time."

Slocum grunted. He didn't much like being dependent on this kid, but he trusted him. This was not Slocum's country. He knew no one, and at least they were well off the trails. A posse wouldn't like that much, three thousand greenbacks or no.

They tended their horses first. Wind seemed to appreciate the shade of the shed, and stood hipshot, resting.

The cabin had a dirt floor, a sheet-iron stove, a table, two chairs, and a single bunk.

"You can take the bunk," Fancher offered.

Slocum shook his head. "I'll sleep out yonder." He pointed to the cottonwoods. "Isn't so stuffy."

"Supposin' it rains?"

"In Kansas, in August?"

"Well, it might."

Slocum studied his young companion. "Be damned if you aren't the most stubborn human being I've come across in a long, long while," he said.

"I feel like a hog, taking the bunk."

"Did it ever occur to you it would be best to split up at night in case we got visitors?"

"Oh!"

"Yes," said Slocum. "Oh! Now, let's see what we got to eat."

"Seems like I'm always putting my foot in the cow pies."

"Yep."

Fancher was chagrined, and searched the cabin for grub silently, almost pouting.

"Listen," said Slocum, "you got nerve, see? Rushing

into the Varieties and telling Ponca he was a rustler took nerve. I admire that. It's exactly what I was going to do."

Fancher's face lightened. "You were?"

"Yeah, I was as much a damn fool as you, so don't worry about it."

Fancher grinned, but said, "I want my cows back. Those bastards got my cows, and I know it."

"What makes you so sure?"

"I had two herds rustled. Each time, there was a cowboy, not the same man, on my payroll who later turned up in Blake's company—and Blake works for Ponca. Now maybe once, if I see a cowboy who worked for me with Blake, that's coincidence. But not twice. Those people were spying for Blake. When the time was right, he let Blake's men know."

Fancher's deductions were similar to those entertained by Slocum. He nodded.

"I'm not a big rancher," Caleb Fancher went on. "Hell, my place is small. But no rancher is too small for Blake. He talked me into selling to him, and when the herd was in the right place, he thieved them." Fancher banged a fist into the palm of his hand. "He does that to all the ranchers around here. Like me, they fall for his smooth talk. He's a great talker, that fellow."

Slocum gave a nod to that, too. Blake had certainly pulled the wool over his own eyes, with his talk about percentages for a successful drive. Ten percent of the gross price for the herd, he had said, and the herd was worth at least twenty-five thousand dollars. Blake had dangled a big carrot in front of Slocum's nose, and he'd followed along like a donkey.

They found the grub easily. There was a sack of beans hanging from a wire attached to a beam and a sack of rice wired in the same way.

"Keeps the stuff safe from mice and other varmints," said Fancher.

They found some coffee in a five-gallon can and also

some tea. Slocum still had some grub in his saddlebags, but Fancher had nothing.

"I wasn't expecting to go on a camping trip," he said wryly.

They would have plenty to eat. There was enough grub to last a month, but, Slocum admitted, they'd get danged tired of rice and beans. It might keep body and soul together, but beans did something to his guts that shouldn't happen to a dog.

Neither of them carried a rifle, but Fancher's .44 packed enough wallop to down an antelope the second day. That shot was fired only after they scoured the countryside to make sure there were no "visitors," as Slocum termed them. A shot's booming could be heard for miles across the silent flatlands.

They took turns standing guard. It was a safety measure, but it also helped pass the time. Each felt he was doing something constructive. When they weren't standing guard, they tried cooking the beans and rice in different ways for variety—boiled, baked, cold, and hot, even fried, though Slocum had to draw the line at fried rice.

"Even if it's done in antelope fat," he said, picking his teeth with a sliver of wood, "it just doesn't seem like a hell of a lot."

There was a pack of worn cards left by the last cowboy who had spent time in the shack, and they played blackjack, stud poker, draw, seven-up—anything they could think of to crack up the hours.

The walls were lined with newspapers to keep out the winter's cold. There were newspapers on the ceiling, too. Slocum read the walls first, as did Fancher. It was old news, the papers being several years of age. A drover was killed in Dodge City and robbed in plain sight. A buyer announced he would give top dollar for any and all beef— longhorns and whitefaces.

"Whitefaces!" exclaimed Fancher, when he read the word. "That's what my cattle were. Good breed, easier to handle than longhorns, and better meat. I should have got at least ten thousand for my beef." He banged his fist into his hand again, a habit he had when agitated. "I wonder who the poisonous snake was who tipped Blake off this time? I pay a man good wages and he turns traitor."

"You pay peanuts," said Slocum mildly.

"What do you mean? I pay as good as any rancher around, and I give a bonus to them as stays the whole drive."

"Blake pays five times as much for just a few words."

"Say, whose side are you on? Sometimes you talk like you envy those thieves."

"Are we having an argument?" Slocum asked dryly.

Fancher stopped his tirade, and flushed. "Hell," he muttered, "I don't mean what I'm saying. I'm getting bushy. Too long out here."

Slocum knew what his friend meant. At the end of three weeks, they had had enough of each other. The very sound of the other's voice was irritating. They were safe where they were—Caleb had been right in that—but they were also so isolated that they hadn't even heard a coyote in a week. No coyote would get so far from humanity, Slocum figured. He'd want to be near cattle and garbage dumps for plenty of feed.

To help pass the time, Slocum taught Fancher something about drawing his pistol. "You looked like you were clawing for crabs that night in the Varieties," Slocum said with more than a touch of sarcasm.

Fancher flushed, but stood up for himself.

"There aren't any crabs around here," he defended. "Hell, the ocean's over a thousand miles away."

Slocum looked his friend over in genuine wonder. "Kid," he said gently, "it's amazing sometimes, just amazing, how little you know of life in the West."

Fancher stared, then reddened again.

"Oh," he muttered, *"those!"*

But Slocum had to give Caleb credit after several days of practice drawing. The object was to draw and shoot in as smooth a motion as possible. Since noise was a danger, they used empty pistols.

"You aren't bad," Slocum admitted. "You wouldn't have a chance against a drunk with no thumbs yet, but you're improving. At least you don't slap leather."

As far as Slocum was concerned, hitting the butt of the pistol so hard it pressed against the holster was a great sin. Drawing and shooting had to be done in one motion, with no interference from the holster, and the young rancher was learning.

"You seem to have the instinct," he told Fancher. "With that, it is just a matter of practice."

"How will I know I'm even going to get it out of the holster when somebody is shooting at me?"

"You don't. Nobody knows that, not even the big ones, but they manage, and so will you. In time."

Slocum's thoughts returned to Marisa at night. He thought of her warm body, her encircling arms. His thoughts grew so heated at times, his longing so intense, that he was forced to walk it off. Once he took a bath in the creek at two in the morning. The creek was cold, and turned his mind from things that couldn't happen, because Marisa was miles and miles away. He wondered if she ever thought of him. If she did, was it the same for her? Did he get so heated up because she was thinking of him at the same time? Slocum had heard of mental telepathy, but he put little stock into it. Yet . . . some time, he'd have to ask her.

He wondered, too, if she was all right. Had anybody seen Wind behind her house? If so, had word got back to Ponca and Blake? Had they come knocking?

Slocum's green eyes hardened when he thought that Marisa might be in danger. He would kill anybody who tried to get tough with her. Anybody at all.

At the end of the third week, when boredom was doing its best to drive them both out of their minds, Slocum had a sudden idea.

"You say your brand was the Square U?" he asked Fancher after the seventh game of stud had ground to a close.

"Yep. Why?"

"An easy brand to doctor."

"Well, yeah, I guess so."

"I wonder if they've been shipped yet."

"How in hell would I know?"

"You wouldn't, but my guess is they haven't. Ponca and Blake have been busy, and they're sending their beeves through Ellsworth only, I think. At least, they've picked the Kansas Pacific for their cargo. I'll bet your herd is still around, waiting its turn. A lot of it, anyway. And if it is, we can turn this around."

"What are you talking about?"

"I'm talking about leaving here and heading for Ellsworth."

"You're crazy."

"We can't stay forever, friend. You know that."

"Yeah. But we'll be recognized."

"We got three, four weeks of whiskers now. By the time we reach Ellsworth, we'll have enough hair on our faces to sell patent medicines. If we're careful, I think we can pass unnoticed for a while."

"What about Wind? There aren't that many spotted horses around."

"No, but there's a few." Slocum was exasperated. "Say, do you want to get out of this mess and maybe get some of your cows back or not?"

"Hell, yes, but . . ."

"You don't take a chance, you don't learn to dance."

Fancher nodded. "All right," he said. "What's your plan?"

"You'll find out soon enough," Slocum told him. "Will you play along?"

"Haven't got a choice, have I?" was the sulky reply.

"No, except I can tell you this much. We got to go to work for the Kansas Pacific Railroad."

"Hell," spewed Fancher, "I don't know a damned thing about railroads."

"You'll learn," said Slocum dryly.

12

Slocum saddled and mounted Wind the next morning to catch the cool breezes at dawn. Fancher rode at his side on Whiskey. Neither man spoke much. A breakfast of boiled rice and coffee had fueled the furnace, but it hadn't done much for the spirit.

"I could use a meal of hotcakes, ham and eggs, toast, steak, fried potatoes, and green peas," grumbled young Caleb. "All washed down with coffee and cream, damn it."

Slocum glanced through the growing light at his side-kick. He was amused. "Peas?" he asked. "Peas for breakfast?"

"Sure, why not!" retorted the other defensively.

"Well, most people would consider peas for lunch or dinner. I haven't heard many people have them for breakfast."

"Well, you don't know everything," was the grumbled reply, and Fancher lapsed into a gloomy silence.

But Slocum, who was having fun, wouldn't let his companion seek the doubtful comforts of gloom. "You're not very sociable in the morning," he said. "I've noticed that. When you get married, your wife will expect you to be more lively, even pleasant. I didn't expect it, partner. With me, it's every man for himself, and he can treat the morning just the way he wants. But you take a wife . . ."

"I ain't getting married!" snarled Fancher. "Shut up about it, will you?"

"Now, is that any way to talk to a feller who has only got your own best interests at heart? Didn't I get all those prairie dogs for you, which you loved so much?"

"Oh, for God's sake, Slocum, how could you eat those greasy little bastards? Tough as leather, not fit for humans."

"You bring God's name into this? All right, let me tell you something: God put all creatures on earth to serve each other. Those little creatures were put in our reach so we could catch them without wasting powder and lead. It was God's way of saying, 'Eat hearty in safety.' You'll notice he didn't send us any more antelope after the one we got."

Caleb Fancher spat. "I never tasted any meat so miserable as those dogs. And you hunted them like a savage."

"I am a savage," said Slocum mildly. "And the way I hunted them was the best way, just waiting on top of their holes until they stuck their heads out, then conking them. Too many pistol shots send out wide circles of sound."

Slocum knew what was really getting to Caleb. It wasn't the prairie dogs, nor was it Slocum's teasing about marriage. It was the uncertainty of the coming days. Would they be caught in Ellsworth? Would Fancher get his cattle back? Would he, indeed, be able to recover from the loss of the herd, and continue as a rancher, if he didn't get them back? These were troublesome questions, questions that gnawed at a man's spirit.

Slocum was just damned glad to leave that line shack behind. They both had a strong case of cabin fever. In another week, they'd have been at each other's throats. Slocum had seen it happen before, even in the War. People just weren't made to be cooped up. That damned cabin had gotten mighty small the past several days. At least he had slept out in the open, been able to get out alone at night and look at the stars for comfort.

They rode in silence. Slocum, with Fancher's help since he knew the country better, had estimated they had a four-day journey to Ellsworth. They were heading west toward the Chisholm, and would push north when they hit it. It was going to be a long trip, and that in itself didn't bring joy to Caleb's life.

"God," he muttered, "I wish they had something faster than horses."

"Maybe people will grow wheels in a hundred years or so," Slocum offered, his eyes glinting. Fancher was so humorless at times.

"Balls," uttered Fancher ungraciously.

Again they rode in silence. The relentless Kansas sun soaked the sweat out of them until their shirts were plastered to their backs and their eyebrows dripped salt into their eyes.

"How long before we hit the Chisholm?" Slocum asked when the sun was overhead.

Fancher scrutinized the country.

"An hour, maybe two," he said. Then he added, "I think I got a right to know what your plan is. After all, I'm in this pretty deep, you know."

"I'll tell you when I'm ready," was the short reply.

Slocum believed in the power of secrecy. One man kept a secret. Two no longer had a secret. It wasn't that he didn't trust Caleb, but there was always the horrible chance that the young rancher could be captured by the law—or, worse, by Paul Meers. Meers would want to know all about Slocum and what was going on. He wouldn't take no for an answer, and there were ways to make people talk.

Whites had picked up Indians' torture methods. The less Fancher knew, the less he could spill if worse came to worst.

Reacting to Slocum's curt reply, Fancher again lapsed into a sullen silence.

Slocum paid little attention to Caleb's moods. He liked the man. The rancher had guts and he had ambitions, and he was willing to work. He would be a hard worker, though short-tempered and sullen, sometimes, all of his life. But, Slocum felt, he would also be a loyal friend—a man who would fight for another—and that was the kind of man Slocum admired.

They reached the Chisholm Trail in ninety minutes from the time Slocum had posed the question. He complimented Fancher. "You sure know this country, friend."

Fancher smiled. He was pleased by the compliment, and he also felt good to be on the main throughway in the country. Ellsworth was only four days away, and once in Ellsworth they could start investigating. He was sure they would turn up something good, and maybe he'd get his cows back.

"Yeah," he said cheerfully. "Well, I guess I do know some things."

"Yes," said Slocum, "you do. And I wonder if you could tell me something else."

"Just ask."

"Who are those four gents coming down on us from the rear?"

Fancher whirled in his saddle. He saw four horsemen galloping swiftly toward them. He stiffened. "I think I saw that first fellow at the Varieties that night," he said.

"I think you did."

"I wonder what they want?"

"Yeah, so do I," Slocum said, with a wry smile breaking on his face.

Slocum checked his Colt quickly. All was well. The caps had been replaced that morning, and the powder was not damp. He loosened the flap on his spare holster.

Fancher witnessed these preparations. "My God," he muttered, "they're bounty hunters."

"You can be quick," said Slocum dryly, "or you can be dead."

But he noted that Caleb checked his .44, and he'd bet now the kid would show some speed.

The four rode to within twenty feet of Slocum and Fancher before the leader raised his hand and they pulled up. They were, thought Slocum, like a small patrol of horse soldiers.

He didn't know any of the men, except for having seen the one, but he typed them at a glance. They were among the wanderers of the plains. They belonged to that band of itinerants who called no place home. They followed the seasons. In summer they hired out on trail drives. In winter they holed up as line riders, or perhaps scraped a living from cards in one of the towns. They were outside the law this year, wore a deputy's badge the next. They owed allegiance to no man, save those with whom they rode at the moment, and they called themselves citizens of no state, territory, or nation. They made a living at whatever turned up, and right now they were looking at three thousand dollars looking back with hard green eyes.

"You Slocum?" asked the leader.

His voice was husky as dead grass rustling and his weathered lips barely moved.

"You know who I am," Slocum replied.

"Yeah."

"So?"

"So I think you better come with us."

Slocum went for his pistol, but an ominous-looking muzzle poked around the quartet's leader, freezing his hand.

"Don't," said the owner of the muzzle, a man who had remained slightly hidden by the leader. The man reined his horse into full sight. "We can take you into Dodge dead or alive." He shrugged. "It wouldn't make a bit of difference t' us." He grinned without mirth. " 'Cept for the smell, maybe. It's three days to Dodge."

Slocum cursed himself for his carelessness. He should have noticed the man's hidden gun hand and nudged Wind into a position from which he could see better.

"Just drop your gunbelts," said the leader. "Go very slow, Slocum." He indicated his men. They had all drawn their weapons now. "You can't beat two pair of .44s."

"You can go to hell!" cried Caleb Fancher truculently. "You're not taking me in!"

"Oh, but we are," the leader assured him. "They's a thousand on your head, too." When he saw Fancher's surprise, he added amiably, "Didn't you know? That's for your part in killing poor old Carp."

"He was going to kill *me!*" Fancher declared. "He got what was coming to him."

The other nodded. "Maybe. It ain't for me to say. Now, then," he went on as he thumbed the hammer back on his pistol, "you going to do like I say?"

Fancher glanced at Slocum angrily, but did as he was told.

Slocum, meanwhile, had been taking his friend's objections in with interest. Had he himself ever been so bold? No. Had he ever been so reckless in the face of sure death? Maybe. Maybe a long time ago, in the War, and maybe when he first came west and the War's bitterness was still a guiding factor in his life. But surely he'd outgrown such crazy behavior by now. God helped the young. Certainly he helped the brash rancher and cowboy, Caleb Fancher.

But as Slocum made these observations, his eyes were detailing fact. They sent these facts to Slocum's brain, and told him this:

The leader held a Walker percussion .44, a hefty weapon. What the leader didn't know was that a cap was missing on the next chamber. Could it be a cap was miss-

ing from the chamber under the hammer as well? Could he
grab the Walker without getting shot?

Such were the slim margins upon which life sometimes
stood. You gambled with the odds, and if you made it, life
went on. If you didn't . . .

Slocum didn't take long to make up his mind. He had
no choice, since he was going to be a dead man anyway.
The four would probably ride them to within half a day of
Dodge, then shoot them as a precaution against escape.
That way the smell would not be a problem. Even if they
were taken all the way to Dodge alive, they would eventually hang.

Slocum acted. He suddenly charged into the man with
the Walker and grabbed the pistol just as the hammer fell.
Click! There was no orange flash, no blast of gunpowder,
no white cloud of smoke.

The two wrestled only for a moment to control the
weapon, before Slocum brought his powerful muscles to
bear. He drove a short chop into the man's jaw, smashing it
with bruising knuckles. The blow made a sound like a
board cracking and the man crumpled, his eyes rolling into
the back of his head. He went off his horse like a sack of
sugar beets and hit the dirt with a muffled crunch. Slocum
crowded Wind into the other three, and their horses shied.
Guns went off, popping like a string of Chinese fire-
crackers, but the bullets whistled harmlessly into the air.

Fancher, recovering quickly from the swiftness of Slocum's attack, charged into the three. He knocked one man
from his horse with a hand calloused by rope work. Then
he plunged into another, just as the man's weapon roared.
Whiskey, Fancher's sorrel, shuddered and gave out a whin-
nying cry of pain. The horse reared up on his hind legs,
and then fell over heavily on his side. Fancher barely managed to kick free of the stirrups. In falling, Whiskey
knocked into a bounty hunter's horse, throwing him sideways, unbalancing the rider. Fancher grabbed the man and

pulled him off his horse, while at the same time coming down with a hard blow on the fellow's neck. The man folded up.

Slocum had not been idle. The advantage of surprise was to follow through. It was a lesson he'd learned long before, and he didn't waste a second. He knew instinctively what had to be done, and he did it, throwing himself at the remaining pair. He used the barrel of his Colt like a hammer. He drove the butt into one man's nose and saw it burst like a ripe tomato. The man gagged on his own blood and doubled up in agony, out of the action. Slocum drove at the other man, raising his arm and gun hand like an avenging scythe. Then Fancher rushed over to block the man's escape. Slocum connected on the man's pate with a sickening crunch of bone, and between them the fourth man was down and bloody.

Slocum quickly gathered up all the weapons, which included a breech-loading Sharps.

"For long distance," Slocum grunted.

Fancher kneeled at the side of Whiskey. The horse was bleeding from a wound in his chest, and Fancher knew it was mortal.

"God damn it," he said quietly, "you were good, Whiskey. I hate to do this, but I got to, you know."

He placed his .44 to Whiskey's temple and fired. The animal shuddered, then lay still.

Fancher turned to the man who had fired the fatal shot. He levelled his gun on him and cocked the hammer. The bounty hunter shrank back, expecting a bullet. For a long moment, there wasn't a sound. Fancher's face froze into a mask of hatred, and his finger curled toward the trigger like a scorpion's tail.

Slocum pushed Fancher's arm down.

"Don't do it," he suggested. "Don't shoot an unarmed man."

"He killed my best horse. He was a friend."

"And before they got us to Dodge they would have

treated us to the same medicine," said Slocum.

He turned to the four.

"I hate your kind," he said. "You are about as worthless as shit. I should let Fancher shoot all of you, and I should help, but you aren't worth the lead."

He turned to his young friend, whose eyes were still hot with anger and sorrow.

"A lady friend of mine once told me that if you're going to do it, do it right."

"What's right?" growled Fancher.

"This—you keep those boys covered."

While Caleb levelled his pistol at the four, who stood in a line about three feet apart, obeying Slocum's instructions, Slocum unsaddled three of their horses. Then he whopped the animals on their rumps and fired a couple of shots in the air. The horses galloped off; they picked up speed, until they were streaking across the flatlands like racers.

"Hey," shouted the leader of the bounty men, "how we going to get anywheres? We'll die out here without our horses."

"Aw," said Slocum with a wicked grin.

"You take that last bronc there," he said to Fancher. "He'll get you to where we are going. You can sell him for another mount if you want to."

The horse looked a bit like Whiskey, light brown with a dark mane. Fancher nodded, stripped his own saddle off the body of Whiskey, and threw it on his new mount.

"Maybe I'll keep him," he said bitterly, "in payment. Maybe I'll keep him and call him Whiskey."

As his last act, Slocum made the four men take off their boots, and put them in a pile. A little dry grass and some twigs under them blazed when Slocum applied a match. The boots, some dry and cracked, others well-oiled and glistening, burned to char, while their owners watched in horror.

"Now we can't even walk," one complained.

"A damned shame, ain't it?" leered Fancher, finally part

of Slocum's wry game.

Gathering up all their canteens except one, Slocum mounted Wind, and Fancher his new Whiskey.

"We'll dry up if you take our water," one of the hunters objected.

Slocum's voice hardened. "You're lucky to have your hide left on your skeletons," he growled. "I ought to have let Fancher here kill all of you. You listen and listen good. If I ever see any of you anyplace at all, I'm going to blow out your brains."

He spit on the ground. "Let's go, Caleb," he said, and the two rode off.

Fancher took one last sad look at Whiskey lying on the ground. "So long," he murmured. "You were a good old hoss."

They never looked back, nor did they speak to each other for the next five miles. Each was occupied with his own thoughts about what had just happened. Each was thinking, too, of the future. Slocum was solidifying his plans to expose Blake and Ponca, and Fancher was still trying to figure out how it would be done. Both were fully aware of the fact that if there had been four bounty hunters, there must be more. Four thousand dollars in cash was hard to pass up. Ambush was entirely possible, and as they rode, the two watched the rolling high-grass country until their eyes burned. They rode through gullies quickly, one looking one way, the other the opposite.

Fancher also wondered about the man he travelled with. He had never known anybody like John Slocum. The man was dangerous. He had killed, yet he was no killer. He was hard, yet there was in him a certain sympathy for the human race. Don't cross him; he'd bring you down. Yet he had just let four bounty hunters, murderers, as Slocum well knew, have a second chance at life. Slocum was an enigma.

Fancher finally broke the silence. "I didn't think we'd make it back there."

"You have to hold a steady rein," said Slocum.

"You do that, don't you?"

"I try."

The two men rode on through the boiling afternoon, their eyes squinting up like fists, their tempers smouldering just below the surface. The next man to face them with a drawn gun was not likely to fare as well as the four bounty hunters, afoot back there in a hell called Kansas.

13

The four days ride to Ellsworth seemed endless. To Slocum, infinity was shorter; to Fancher, it seemed that his whole body had turned against him. Every muscle screamed like a tortured soul in hell.

Slocum was aware that his feelings were based on impatience, but that didn't make the ride any easier. His stomach twisted into knots every time he thought about those bastards who had rustled the cattle he had driven over a thousand miles. He wanted to get to the heart of the matter as quickly as possible. Yet, even after they arrived in Ellsworth, there would be no quick solution. He knew what he had to do, but a succinct question remained: How to do it?

During rest periods, Fancher practiced his fast draw to break the monotony. He admired Slocum's seemingly effortless action, and tried to copy his style.

"Don't do that," Slocum instructed. "You can't copy me, no more than I can copy your Square U brand. You're built different; you have different reflexes. Remember that, Caleb. You have to develop your own style of draw and shoot."

And so Fancher persisted. He improved. He did develop his own style, a sort of crouch and grab.

Slocum sighed. The young man might in time become fair, but never a great draw artist. He was, however, a good shot once he separated hardware from leather.

"Maybe," Slocum advised, "you better settle for putting the bullets where you want them. Not everybody can do that, you know."

Fancher nodded, but he didn't agree. "I'll get there, John. Wait and see."

The two men arrived in Ellsworth after dark. The timing was deliberate. Though the beards on their faces had thickened considerably, they stayed to the shadows like desperadoes, like the wanted men they were.

They rented a hotel room after putting their horses in a stable. In the room, Slocum opened a window and listened to nighttime Ellsworth carefully. Street talk floated to him. A Kansas Pacific engine chuffed near the loading pens. Cows bawled. Laughter drilled the atmosphere, coming through open saloon doors. The shrill voices of women on the prod accompanied the laughter. Slocum measured the temper of the town by its noise. Ellsworth sounded like any other cowtown at night. There was nothing unusual to make him suspicious—no silences, nobody watching the hotel. The town was just as it should be.

A group of liquored-up cowhands emerged from a bar laughing. Slocum watched as they made a turn all together, like a flock of swallows in flight. They were headed for the women in Nauchville.

"Hey," shouted one, "ever hear about the girl who swallowed a pin when she was eleven?"

"Tell us!" cried another.

"She never felt a prick till she was sixteen."

More laughter. Then the horny bunch was gone, and the

bustle of Ellsworth went back to its usual liquid level.

Slocum's face creased with a slow grin. All seemed well. He didn't doubt that Blake and Ponca had given full descriptions of the "desperadoes" to the local marshal by now. Anybody wearing a badge would have to be avoided. Actually, their arrival would not draw much notice. People were arriving in and leaving Ellsworth by the score every day: cowboys, drovers, buyers, settlers—called "grangers" by the locals—drummers, good men and bad were coming and going as commerce dictated, and Ellsworth was booming.

Even so, Slocum wasn't taking any chances. He would have been happy to have remained in the room until the next day, but Caleb Fancher's fuse lit up again.

"Damn it," he complained, "I'm starving. Let's get something to eat."

Slocum had to admit that surrounding a thick steak together with fried potatoes, vegetables, fresh bread, pie, and some good coffee, would be welcome. For weeks he had existed mainly on beans, rice, antelope, and prairie dogs. And the coffee had tasted like something you could clean a gun with. Juices wetted his mouth as he thought about the meal they could have. There was a café across the street, and his nose caught cooking odors, which didn't help his willpower.

"We could be recognized," he warned.

"So what the hell?" philosophized young Fancher.

"All right."

Slocum ordered from a slate set in a wooden frame that itemized the bill of fare at cowtown prices, everything his mind told him his stomach needed. Fancher was close behind, but he didn't order fried potatoes. He ordered a plate of green peas.

"And I don't care if they're fresh or canned," he told the waiter. "Just so's they're hot."

"You and your peas," said Slocum.

"My mother always said to put something green on the

dinner plate," Fancher replied. "Green things are good for you."

"Unless it's mold," Slocum suggested.

"Fuck you, Slocum," said Caleb amiably.

They sat in a shadowed corner, their backs to the wall, a ploy advised by Slocum.

"Just like in those stories I'm reading," said Fancher, pleased with this role.

"What do you mean?" Slocum had never read much about the West, especially the new fictions.

"People on the watch always sit with their backs to the wall," said Caleb.

"Makes sense," grunted Slocum. He dove into his meal after it arrived hot and steaming.

It was good to eat civilized victuals again. It was even nice to hear the bustle of a lively town and see people dressed neatly. And to see women. There were women in the restaurant. They were with escorts, and they wore long dresses, little hats perched primly atop their hair. They weren't Slocum's type, but it had been a long three weeks and more since Marisa. He didn't know how a woman in a long dress and wearing a perky bonnet would be. Under the cool, was there heat?

There was one woman, a young lady not over twenty, who came in unescorted. She was pretty. She had very blue eyes and long blond hair. Her face was finely chiseled, like the faces of Swedish girls Slocum had seen among the new settlers. She sat close to Slocum and Fancher and folded her hands demurely in her lap. The waiter took her order, and it was then she turned to face Slocum directly. Their eyes met, and Slocum was jolted. He knew at once that she recognized him, though he had no idea who she was. She nodded slightly and turned away. All through the meal, Slocum wondered where she knew him from, and why she didn't send for the law. He said nothing to Fancher. There was little use in two of them being puzzled, but he continued to wonder about the girl.

The restaurant had a saloon attached. Occasionally, loud voices and raucous laughter drifted through the open door, disturbing the diners. The noise bothered Slocum, too, so he got up and shut the door. As he did so, he glanced into the barroom. Some railroad men were having a party, and the sight of them sent a tingle of impatience along Slocum's spine. He had come to Ellsworth to work for the Kansas Pacific, and he wanted that job *now*. It was an important part of his plan.

He returned to his table, noticing as he did so that the young blonde's handkerchief had dropped to the floor. He picked it up and handed it to her.

"Yours, ma'am?"

"Thank you," she replied. "How careless of me."

She reached out to take the handkerchief, and as she did so, she deftly shoved a folded paper into Slocum's palm. He closed his hand around it without a break in the courtesies, saluted her with his free hand, and returned to his table.

"You took a chance," hissed Fancher, angry over Slocum's shutting the door.

"Yes, but it's quieter, don't you agree?"

"You do something like that, and yet you tell me that eating out like this is dangerous. I can't figure you, Slocum," the young rancher said.

"I never asked you to."

Slocum slipped the paper into his pocket for later reading. He was certain it was a note.

In the meantime, laughter pounded on the door to the saloon, though muffled now, and as it did so, Slocum thought up his plan. It was crazy, but then, crazy plans sometimes worked, if you believed in them enough, if you were bold enough.

After they had finished eating and had downed hot cups of Arbuckle coffee, they left the restaurant. Slocum caught the blonde's eyes. He didn't know what the note said yet, but he nodded, and she gave him a quick smile.

When they were back in the room, Slocum read the note. It said, simply, "Meet me at the schoolhouse tonight."

No salutation, no signature—just one terse sentence.

Fancher saw the paper. "What's that?" he asked.

Slocum showed it to him, and told him how he came to have it.

Fancher whistled. "Jesus, the women are after you and you don't even know them. She was a mighty fine-looking girl, too."

"I think she has other things on her mind."

Fancher nodded. "Yeah, I wonder what?"

"We'll find out soon."

"Want me to come along?"

"No. If I'm caught, if this is some kind of a trap, at least you'll still be free."

The rancher nodded, seeing the logic, and Slocum left.

His knowledge of Ellsworth wasn't as detailed as his knowledge of Dodge, but he did know where the schoolhouse was. Keeping to the darker edges of town, he made his way, and soon came up on the plain board building. He approached cautiously. Was this a trap? Or did the girl, who seemed to know him, have something else in mind? Slocum found himself wishing that she had on her mind what he had on his, but dismissed the wish as unlikely.

He looked through the window and saw the girl's silhouette. She was sitting at a desk, and was outlined against a far window. She was full-breasted. Her breasts' size seemed exaggerated by the shadow's illumination. Or were they? Slocum fought his thoughts. This was no time for either love or lust. She might be the spider and he the fly.

After a quick scrutiny, Slocum saw no danger. That didn't mean danger wasn't lurking, but he decided to take a chance. That young woman wanted to see him very much.

She had recognized him, but she hadn't sent for the marshal, so if there was danger, Slocum couldn't pin it down. He checked his Colt to see that it was ready, then knocked on the window.

The girl glanced up quickly, then went to the door. Slocum met her there and entered. She shut the door behind him and locked it.

"Anybody see you?" she asked.

Slocum liked the sound of her voice. It was soft and low.

"No," he answered.

"Come."

She led the way to a back room. Slocum was surprised to recognize it as an apartment, probably where she lived. Most teachers boarded with the parents of students.

She sensed his surprise. "I like my privacy," she explained. "They gave these quarters as a condition to my teaching here."

"It's nice," said Slocum. "Now, what did you want to see me about?"

"Blake and Ponca."

Slocum had expected something of the sort. He wasn't sure just what, but her direct answer startled him. This girl didn't waste time.

"My name," she said, "Is Merry Lynn Adams. I know you are John Slocum, and I don't feel so merry just now."

"How did you know I'm Slocum?"

"I saw you in Dodge when you shot that horrible man, Carp."

"It was regrettable."

"No, it wasn't. He had it coming."

Silence filled the space between them. It was Merry Lynn Adams's party, and Slocum was going to let her serve the wing-dings.

"I was Blake's fiancée," said Merry suddenly.

"I see," Slocum replied. *"Was?"*

"He left me for Ponca's sister," said Merry with anger. "He left me cold for Vernine, and do you know what she does?"

"No."

"She runs a whorehouse. It's called Sally's. Do you know the place?"

"Should I?"

"I thought you might."

Merry's voice was matter-of-fact. She wasn't sliding into innuendo. Slocum's sexual activities weren't the point.

"I've heard of it. I didn't know Ponca's sister ran it," he told her.

"He's a hateful man. It was because of him I lost Blake." The voice took on a husky timbre. "I loved Blake, and I still do, Slocum, but I can't stand him for what he did to me—deserting me for a common *whore!* I could understand it better if she were a normal woman, but a *whore?*"

Merry had not lit the kerosene lamp, for which Slocum was grateful. Darkness concealed, and it also brought intimacy. He felt Merry's physical closeness, was very much aware of her large breasts and lovely face, only half visible in the dim light. They were standing facing each other. Merry hadn't suggested sitting.

"I hate him, and I'm going to tell you something: Blake and Ponca are in partnership. They have a cattle deal going on that is making them thousands, and those cattle are rustled."

The girl wasn't telling Slocum anything he didn't already know, but her substantiation of his suspicions helped strengthen his reasoning.

"How do you know?" he asked.

"Blake told me himself. He trusted me. He told me a lot. How could he desert me the way he did—to please Ponca, maybe?"

She was almost hissing in anger. Slocum said nothing.

"When Blake first arrived in town, he was broke. We met at a dance and fell in love. At least *I* fell in love. Well, there was nothing here for him, so he went to Dodge. I didn't know he was a gambler, and I'll give him this: He didn't want to embarrass me, so he went to Dodge. I understand he made money at it. He caught Ponca's eye and the two formed a partnership. Damn that Ponca! Blake suddenly came into a lot of money, and I know where it comes from. He gets back here now and then, and he even drops in on me, but he spends his nights with Vernine!"

After that outburst, the girl was silent.

"What I'm looking for is proof," said Slocum. "I know you're right about Ponca and Earl Blake, but I have no proof.

"You want proof? Take a look at some of the shipping manifests. See who is sending the cattle and to whom."

The light went on in Slocum's mind. Of course! This was the key he'd been looking for. This was the key that would open secret doors. But how to get to those manifests? One didn't just demand them—especially not John Slocum, who was wanted by the law. He didn't dare make himself conspicuous by walking into the KP shipping office and asking to see them. There had to be another way.

Merry was crying, and Slocum did what he always did when a woman was in tears and practically leaning on his chest. He took her in his arms. The girl snuggled up against his large frame, her tears flowing.

"Don't let that fellow upset you so," he whispered. "He isn't worth it."

"But the stupid thing is I still love him."

"I thought you said a minute ago that you hated him."

"That, too," admitted Merry Lynn.

Slocum didn't try to figure it out. He never tried to figure women out, because it was an exercise in futility. But he began to feel the weeping girl's body heat, and his need for a woman began to show.

"Damn him," Merry swore angrily, wiping away the tears with the back of her hand, "just damn him."

Slocum didn't try to figure women out, but he did know

a thing or two. One thing he knew was that a woman scorned was apt to be vengeful. And one of the ways they sometimes sought to even scores was by taking a lover. He pressed the girl closer and she responded. Her large, full breasts caressed his chest through the cloth of his shirt.

"Damn him," she said softly.

Slocum kissed her, and she returned his kiss with fierce passion. There was a bed against one wall, and Slocum led her to it. They sat side by side, their lips touching, brushing, but not kissing. Slocum cupped a clothed breast in his large hand.

"Let's undress," he said.

Merry was out of her layers of clothing before he was shed of his simpler garments of boots, socks, trousers, and shirt. She stood before him, eyes shining, her breasts inches from his lips. Slocum slipped a hand between her thighs and slid it upward slowly, while at the same time he pressed his lips to her flat stomach.

"My God!" she gasped.

Merry collapsed on the bed, and Slocum mounted her. He spread her legs apart, and sought the moist target with his throbbing lance.

"You're so big," she whispered. "So big!"

Slocum kissed the girl. He ground into her, and she, awakened to desire, fought back, and when he came, his senses reeled with the sensation. She came immediately after he did, and she clawed his bare back in the hot hunger of her lust.

When it was over, they rested in each other's arms. They slept, but sleep was brief, for each was in great need, and they sensed this might be the only night they would have together.

Just before dawn, Slocum dressed.

"I'm going to kill her," said Merry Lynn Adams.

"Who?" asked Slocum, his body entirely relaxed, his mind not so quick as a few hours before.

"That bitch Vernine Ponca. I want more than what you

gave me last night. I want revenge, Slocum. I want her life."

The girl spoke with such bitter conviction that Slocum knew she meant it.

"Be careful," he warned gently. "Killing somebody isn't as easy as it seems. The sort of revenge you had with me is one thing, but to kill is something else."

"I'm going to get her," said Merry, ignoring the advice. "She took my man, and the price is going to be high."

"Don't do anything," said Slocum. He kissed the girl. "I've got to go before daylight. I'll try to see you again soon."

Merry nodded, and returned his kiss, but she repeated her words. "I'm going to kill Vernine Ponca."

14

"Where you been?" growled Fancher when Slocum returned as dawn slit the eastern horizon with pale light.

"Making plans," said Slocum.

"With who? That woman?" Fancher shook his head. "You must think I'm some kind of a dunce."

"Well, you said it."

The rancher flushed. "Hey," he muttered, "I'm not prying. I just don't know what to expect. For all I knew you were a dead man, and they were looking for me next."

"Scary," admitted Slocum, "but, no, I'm very much alive. Now for some sleep."

Caleb slouched down in the bed, and Slocum joined him. This was a one-bed room, and they had to make do. One slept where one could.

Slocum sank quickly into a deep sleep. Caleb rolled a cigarette and smoked it slowly. He was impatient. He wanted to get something done, but he had to wait for Slocum. Slocum had the plan.

129

Slocum slept until mid-morning, waking up fresh. The night's loving had done him good. He felt whole again, once more like John Slocum. A man needed what only a woman could give to keep the balance, or he began to dry up somewhere inside, like wheat stubble. A romp in the hay was a tonic, and with a girl like Merry Lynn Adams, a shot of good bourbon had been mixed in.

They chanced another meal at the café across the street. They could read the name on the false front now: Mary's Eatery. The clientele seemed to be local, the diners a cut above the cowhands who ate at saloons and greasy spoons. Slocum studied the people who came through the door. He had never seen such a variety, but one thing satisfied him: They were all intent on their own business.

After breakfast, he said to Fancher, "Let's go into the bar."

"A drink at this hour?" Caleb shuddered.

"Just come on, and stop throwing obstacles in my way all the time."

Slocum liked Fancher, but the man could be exasperating.

They entered the saloon next door, which seemed to be under a different proprietorship. As Slocum had hoped, there were railroad men present. He guessed they were off shift and getting their drinking done now. Mid-morning was mid-night to them. He strolled over to the bar and took a stool next to two KP men who were more than a little into their cups. Fancher sat down beside him, wondering why they were there.

Slocum ordered drinks for the house, and included himself and Fancher in the round.

"Thanks, stranger," said one of the men. "Name's Lem. All drinks are welcome. Here's how."

They were drinking whiskey, straight, with beer.

"You boys looked thirsty," said Slocum. "Always glad to help out a couple of trainmen. We bring up the cattle, you haul 'em to market. In a way, we're partners."

"Yeah," said Lem. "Never thought about that."

"Aren't you supposed to be at the yards today?"

"Naw, we just got in last night, so's we got a couple of days off. We hit the pens tomorrow morning. Right, Petey?"

Petey, the second man in the pair, raised his glass and grinned. He was missing a front tooth, and the grin seemed double-wide. He didn't say anything, just downed his whiskey, made a face, and took a quick sip of beer.

"How's a fellow get a job on the trains?" Slocum asked.

"Why, hell, man, you just go to the timekeeper's office down by the pens. If there's anything, he'll let you know." He looked Slocum over with a bleary eye. "Wouldn't of thought you'd be innersted in train work."

"My partner and me, we just want to see how it works on the other side."

Lem nodded wisely. "Makes sense," he said. "Go see the timekeeper."

"Thanks."

Once outside, Fancher asked, "Now what is this all about? I don't want to work for no railroad! I thought you were joking back at the line cabin. Hell, I'm a rancher."

"You *were* a rancher," Slocum reminded him. "Right now you got a ranch house but no cows, so that makes you a homesteader. We got to get on the inside somehow so we can look at records. The best way, unless you want to break into the office, is going to work for the KP. Maybe we'll get our chance."

"So that's your plan!"

"Part of it."

"What's the other part?"

Slocum debated whether or not he should tell Fancher the whole plan. The youth was so excitable that he decided against it for the moment.

He shook his head. "Give it time, Caleb. Give it time."

The timekeeper, a skinny fellow wearing spectacles that had slid down to the tip of his long nose, was not encouraging.

"Ain't nothing now," he said. "Mebbe in a week or two, when they put on more cars before winter comes." He looked at them curiously. "Know anything about train work?"

"No, but we know cows and how to get 'em into the boxcars," said Slocum.

The timekeeper nodded. "All right. Try us again in a couple of weeks."

They headed back for the main part of town. Fancher was worried. "What now?"

"I figured that was the answer we'd get. I'm prepared for it. Now we follow through with the rest of it."

"What's that?"

"First we get another meal, a good greasy one."

Young Caleb stared. "We just had enough breakfast for a platoon. Why more?"

"We'll just have coffee, Caleb. Don't worry about it. You'll see."

On their way to the restaurant, Slocum saw Merry across the street. She looked at him, but made no effort to send a greeting. Instead, she looked away, and strode with determined steps down the walk. Slocum knew that Sally's was in that direction, and he wondered. Was more revenge about to take place?

He watched the girl. She was wearing a long coat, odd for a warm August day, and she walked queerly, sort of stiff-legged.

"You go to the hotel room and wait for me," he said to Fancher.

"But what about that coffee? I could use some after that whiskey."

"It can wait."

He left Fancher scratching his head and walked across the street.

"Oh," Fancher called after him, "I get it." There was both disgust and envy in his voice. He had not yet had a woman, and his feelings were on the rise in the matter. Slocum didn't answer, and Fancher watched Slocum's broad, muscular back as it disappeared around a corner.

Sure, he thought, *he gets all the fun, while I roost in that damned room like a chicken. Hell.* But he stomped off to the room to wait. Slocum held all the cards—or at least he had the best hand. In the room, Fancher practiced his fast draw. It seemed to him he was getting better.

Slocum caught up with Merry and fell in alongside her. She glanced at him. "I don't need you for this, John."

"I think you do."

"No. Go away, now. This is private."

Slocum stepped in front of the girl, and she stopped. He reached into her coat and withdrew a twin-barrelled shotgun. He shot out a muscular wrist and grasped the barrels with his hand. She struggled for possession momentarily, but she was no match for Slocum, and he snatched it out of her hands.

"Going out for a few prairie chickens?" he asked pleasantly. He glanced at the sky, a deep blue, and the sun, a bright yellow. "Nice day for an outing."

"You know damn well where I'm going," said Merry angrily.

"Yes, I know, and I still say, don't."

"She has it coming."

"Maybe. Maybe not."

"She took Blake from me."

"Ever think that she didn't take him, but he went to her?"

Merry was suddenly uncertain. "Damn you, John," she said fiercely. "Why are you doing this?"

"That's not a nice way for a schoolteacher to talk."

"Why are you doing this?"

"To keep you from hanging."

Merry looked startled.

"Didn't think of that, did you?" he asked.

"She took my man."

"In the eyes of the law, murder knows no excuses. You'll hang."

"Then I'll hang!" cried Merry Lynn Adams. "But at least I'll get her."

"Not this morning, you won't."

"Give me back my gun," Merry demanded. She made a grab for it.

Slocum tucked it behind his back. "No chance."

Merry, frustrated, flushed, and didn't seem to know just where to go or what to do.

"Go home," Slocum suggested gently. "It's over."

"No," said Merry, "it is only over for now. I'll get her. You'll see."

She turned and stalked off.

"Shall I call on you tonight?" Slocum asked.

She turned back, her eyes hot with anger and humiliation. "Don't ever come back. I have another one of those," she said, pointing at the shotgun, "and I'll use it on you."

Slocum let her go. He kept the shotgun and walked to Sally's with it. It was the kind of bordello where one knocked to gain entry. Slocum knocked. There was no answer. He knocked again, loudly. This time he heard a stirring inside, and after a few moments a woman opened the door.

"Yes?" she said sleepily.

"I'm looking for Vernine Ponca."

The woman's eyes, brown and soft, were suddenly interested. They appraised Slocum swiftly. He had the feeling she could assess the size of his pocketbook with those eyes in a second. She was about thirty, he guessed, with dark hair, and a nice figure under her gown.

"I don't know you," she said, "but I'm Vernine. What do you want? It's too early for business, cowboy."

"You know somebody named Merry Adams?"

"Sure. She's the schoolteacher."

"You know somebody named Earl Blake?"

The eyes narrowed. "Maybe. I know lots of people."

"Merry wanted to give you this." Slocum brought the shotgun into view. "For Blake."

The madam of Sally's gasped. "My God!"

"You were very close to going up to that happy brothel in the sky this morning."

"But why?"

"You took Merry's man."

"Blake?"

"Right."

"I didn't *take* him. He comes to see me sometimes. He's a friend of my brother's, so I'm nice to him, is all."

"That's not what Merry thinks."

"Well, she can damned well think what she wants. I have no interest in that man."

Just then a male voice called out, "Who is it, Vernine?"

Slocum recognized the voice of Lew Ponca.

This was no place for him. He handed the shotgun to Vernine, saying, "You better keep this. I'd break it in two, if I were you."

He tipped his hat and was gone. He headed for the hotel, wondering about a man who would let his sister whore for a living. Greed. The more you got, the more you wanted, and prostitution was a profitable business.

Fancher was in no better mood than before. "Well," he asked sarcastically, "are you *satisfied* now? Didn't take you long."

"Quit behaving like a kid," Slocum told him in an even, but impatient voice. "I just kept somebody from becoming a cottonwood blossom."

"What?"

"Never mind. Now come on. We have work to do."

At Mary's Eatery, they drank their coffee slowly. Slocum wanted to give the men in the saloon time to go through their pay, get good and liquored up. He sat where he could look through the door and see the men at the bar.

"This doesn't make any sense," said Fancher after Slocum ordered second cups of coffee.

"It will," said John. The noise from the saloon told him the men were getting drunk. He took his time with the second cup. The railway men were not going anywhere, not as long as the booze held out and they had money in their overalls.

The trainmen were still present, and greeted Slocum and Fancher with cheers.

"We feel like a party," said Slocum. "Mind if we join you?"

"Hell, no! Bartender, set 'em up."

At two in the afternoon, Slocum sent Fancher back to the hotel.

"Sleep it off," he told him in private. "We got to be fresh tomorrow."

"All right."

For once Caleb didn't argue. He'd had all the whiskey he could stand and then some. He was glad to get out of it. Whatever in hell Slocum's plan was, it could sink or swim. He could not have cared less.

Slocum didn't drink on each and every round. Complaining of a stomach pain, he skipped, but bought plenty for his new friends, Lem Maginnis and Petey O'Reilly. They were capable of holding a lot. They downed glass after glass, while Slocum watched them with narrowed green hawk eyes. He kept buying and they kept drinking. But every man had his limit, he knew. If he didn't go broke first, the two Irishmen would reach theirs before long.

The day began to fade, and most of the others in the saloon went next door for supper, or to their homes. Slocum kept buying drinks. He could see that the two men would not make it through the next hour. Their speech began to slur and their eyes turned red and watery. By now the bartender was serving them rotgut and charging the higher price. A look passed between him and Slocum. Slocum, pretending to be drunk, shrugged in a sign of secret collaboration.

"Think we ought to call it a night," said Lem, for it was growing dark. "Long day tomorrow."

"Just one more to say so long," Slocum suggested. He didn't want to lose these two. The second part of his plan was nearly complete, but he needed the cooperation of Lem and Petey.

"We got to go to work before sunup," slurred Petey.

"Damned right," said a thick-tongued Lem. "Drunk or sober, we got to be in the yard bright and early o' the mornin'."

"Just one," Slocum said, "for the road."

The boys agreed to one more, and that was the fatal one. Petey went down first, his legs turning to rubber. Lem tried to help his friend up and toppled over.

The bartender laughed. "They lasted longer'n usual," he said.

"You got a back room where my friends can sleep?" Slocum asked the bartender.

"Well . . ."

Slocum slipped the man five dollars.

"Sure, but they. . ."

"I'd be obliged if you would put a lock on this door. I don't want them getting hurt."

"I close at three."

Slocum gave him another five.

"Just go on home, friend," said the big man. "You can let 'em out when you open up in the morning."

"Jiggs opens up at five. These boys have to go to work."

"I'll talk to Jiggs," said Slocum.

The barkeep took the money and helped Slocum lug the drunken men into the storeroom.

After the trainmen were laid out on a couple of cots, Slocum watched as the bartender padlocked the door, shaking his head in puzzlement. Slocum hoped that Lem and Petey would sleep well—for about twelve hours anyway.

He returned to the hotel and slipped into bed without waking Fancher, who slept heavily. At four-thirty he arose, dragged young Caleb from the warm covers, and crossed the street to the saloon.

Jiggs was sweeping up outside.

"We come to fetch Petey and Lem, get 'em to work," said Slocum.

"I wondered was they on today," said the short, rotund man. He had a whiskey nose and red spiderwebs on his cheeks. "Whew-ee, it does fairly reek in that storeroom!"

"What the hell . . . ?" Fancher broke in.

"Shut up," Slocum said amiably.

Back in the storeroom, Caleb held his nose. The sounds of snoring were loud.

"You get Petey. Sling him over your shoulders," said Slocum.

"Damn it, I—"

"Be quick about it," said John, hefting Lem like a grain sack over his broad shoulders.

"We going to take them to work?" asked a dumbfounded Fancher.

"To the yards, but not to work."

"I don't . . ."

"Caleb, these boys are going to catch an eastbound freight. I mean to see they have a nice long trip."

"Well, I'll be goddamned," said Fancher.

After the early freight rolled out of the yards, Slocum and Fancher walked over to the Kansas Pacific timekeeper's shack. No one had seen them as they loaded the two drunks into an empty car just as the train was pulling out. Neither man had awakened.

"I got some news for you," Slocum told the long-nosed man with the pencils.

"Yeah?"

"Lem and Petey won't be in."

"Oh? How come?"

"They've gone to California to look for gold."

"Well, I'll be damned."

"They told us we could have their jobs," Slocum went on. "How about it?"

Fancher nearly choked. "So that's it," he muttered.

"How's that?" asked the timekeeper.

"We need the work," said Caleb earnestly.

"Well, you go see that man there." He pointed to a fellow in a wide-brimmed Stetson who was leaning on one of the pens looking the cows over. "If he says yes, you're on the payroll."

The timekeeper was not a suspicious man. He was a man of facts. Numbers were his game: hours worked and tallies were his expression of life. Yet there was something queer about a couple of cowhands he'd turned down the day before, returning with ready-made jobs. He watched through the window, while the two confronted the Stetson. He saw the big one explaining, and the Stetson exploded. He watched as the pair returned with grins. They were employees of the Kansas Pacific Railroad.

Their duties were numerous, from hooking up boxcars to helping load cattle into them. They tallied while cowboys poked reluctant animals with prods to speed them up ramps.

Slocum didn't need to explain to Fancher what they were looking for. They were looking for the Pollywog—now the Rolling Log—brand, or Fancher's Square U.

"It'll be doctored," said Fancher. "Think we can tell it?"

"My bet is a running iron can make an easy change from Square U to, say, a Line Cabin, or Lean-to."

"Yeah."

They worked a long time in the dust and heat before Fancher spotted a cow with a Lean-to brand. He pointed it out to Slocum.

"And it's a whiteface!" Fancher exclaimed. "I'm willing to bet my life that's one of my critters!"

"You might have to," said Slocum.

Then Fancher said something that reminded Slocum why he liked the young man in spite of his griping.

"I'll go that far if I have to," he said quietly. "You can depend on it."

Slocum nodded. "Now we got to find out two things."

"Please don't keep me in the dark now," said Fancher. "I got a right to know about your plans."

"Part of them, anyway," said Slocum. "Yep, you have that right. We have to find out who is sending them to where, and we have to find out how much the KP is charging."

"How are we going to do that?"

"We'll change uniforms," said John Slocum. "Tomorrow morning."

15

Slocum went to the best haberdashery in Ellsworth. The place sold hats, boots, shirts, and suits—all of better-than-average quality for better-than-average prices.

Slocum selected a suit off the rack which fit well enough. It was brown, tightly woven, and gave off a slight sheen. He also purchased a white shirt, a tie, new boots, and a Stetson. He directed Fancher to do the same. The young rancher did so, mystified.

"Trust me," said Slocum slyly, in a tone that said just the opposite.

After they left the haberdashery, they went to the barbershop, where each had haircuts, and the barber slathered plenty of what Slocum called "stink water" on them.

"Smells pretty good," said Caleb, "actually. But what's the purpose of all this?"

Much to Fancher's frustration, Slocum ignored the question. They returned to the hotel, where Slocum sized himself up in the bureau mirror. He was slightly startled by his clean-shaven face, a face he hadn't seen for a couple of weeks. It was more presentable than he recalled. The rest of him was satisfactory, too. He had become a moneyed buyer from the East—the East being Kansas City or Chicago. He hung his gunbelt around his waist as a finishing touch. Many buyers wore them to guard against robbery, or just to seem like one of the boys in a country where nearly all men who dealt in cattle slung a gun from the hip.

Fancher also passed fair. He was quite pleased with the image he made in the mirror. "I could sure get me a girl now," he said with satisfaction. "Man, I'm pretty."

"You won't get the girl if you are prettier than she is," Slocum warned. "You do look the dandy, though."

"Oh, for God's sake, John, shut up, will you?" Fancher turned crimson. "I just mean that since you are having all the luck with the women around here, it's about my turn."

"We aren't after women, Caleb."

"Well, I know that!" exclaimed the rancher. "Do you take me for a prime fool?" He paused "What *are* we after?"

"We are going to the general offices of the Kansas Pacific Railroad, to learn something. We are cattle buyers. So start acting like one."

Fancher nodded. He drew himself up. Slocum turned away, stifling a laugh.

Slocum led the way to the same building he had visited on his first trip to Ellsworth. They went in and were greeted by a man in a white shirt. Black elastic sleeve holders ringed his upper arms. The fellow with the green eyeshade wasn't present, and Slocum was relieved. That could have made matters sticky, had he been around and recognized the man who had used force.

"Gentlemen?" said the man in the white shirt.

"My name is Curtis," said Slocum, "and this is my associate, Fracas. We are checking beef rates to Kansas City."

"We charge five dollars a head."

Slocum looked at Fancher, alias Fracas, thoughtfully. "What do you think, partner?"

Fancher didn't really know just what to say, since Slocum had not rehearsed him on the details of his plan. He played it safe. "Hmm," he allowed.

"My partner feels those rates are too high. We'll have fifty thousand head to ship by September. We can either go to the Santa Fe in Dodge or use your facilities, but it depends on rates. Sante Fe's offer is four-fifty."

"I'm Dooley," said the white-shirted man, "assistant manager of this station, but I can't make you an offer to match the Santa Fe's."

"Well, then I guess they get our business," Slocum said.

"Did you say fifty thousand head?" Dooley asked.

"Perhaps more, if my plans work out."

"I'll get the general manager, Mr. Jackson."

"You do that," said Slocum. He winked at Fancher, who was taking it all in.

The man disappeared up a flight of stairs. He returned in moments with a heavy, florid man with busy eyes and thinning hair. He was the type, Slocum thought, who acted like a good-time Charley for his company, but who was also shrewd in business matters. Just the kind of man needed for work among a rough-and-tumble crop of cattlemen.

"Come to my office," he invited in a whiskey-mangled voice. "It's more comfortable."

He led the way upstairs to an office with leather-covered chairs, a large oak desk, and big windows overlooking both the KP tracks and the distant pens. He brought out a box of cigars, and offered them. Havanas. Slocum took one, as did Fancher. They lit up, and waited for Jackson to speak.

After a proper interlude, Jackson said, "I understand you will have a number of beeves to ship."

"Fifty thousand, as I told Dooley. Perhaps more."

"Our standard rate to Kansas City is five dollars a head."

"I've heard it said that if there is quantity, the KP will give special rates."

Jackson puffed his Havana. Clouds of white smoke drifted slowly toward the ceiling.

"It is possible," he said finally, "but of course, we can't do that for everybody. What figure did you have in mind?"

"Three seventy-five," was Slocum's cool response.

Jackson laughed. "My dear man!" he exclaimed. "That would never do. You'd lose more than that if you drove them overland just in shrinkage."

"All right." Slocum seemed to give way. "I'll settle for the rate you give Earl Blake."

"Mr. Blake?" Jackson's friendly manner stiffened a bit. "What do you know about him?"

"I know he gets a flat rate of four dollars."

This was it. Slocum had fired his heavy gun. He had no idea how much Blake was paying. He only suspected there was a special rate. Yet the evidence told him there must be. Why would he trail his cattle to the KP instead of the Santa Fe, which was closer? There had to be a reason, and that reason was profit. Slocum had just brought his cannon to bear. It was up to Jackson.

In the meantime, Fancher sat close-mouthed, taking in the proceedings with amazement. If he didn't know Slocum, he would have honestly thought the man had dabbled in such high-power dealings all of his life.

Jackson puffed his cigar again. He twirled it in his fingers and looked at it closely, as if he'd found a flaw in the wrapper leaf.

"My dear Mr. Curtis," he said at length, "I don't know where you get your information . . ."

"From Blake and Ponca," Slocum said. "We do friendly business from time to time."

"Ah, I see."

More puffs. Slocum kept pace, and while so doing, watched Jackson with narrowed, cold eyes. It was a calculated act, meant to unnerve the KP general manager.

"We give them a rate of four and a quarter," said Jackson suddenly, "not four dollars."

"I don't believe it," said Slocum, making his voice as hostile as possible, the better to shake the other man. He glanced at his cigar. "Too bad we can't do business. I like Havanas." He beckoned to Fancher. "Let's hit Dodge. We have a deal there."

He rose.

Jackson rose at the same time, saying, "Wait." He pulled a sheaf of papers from a file. "These are shipping bills for Blake," he said. "See for yourself."

A moment of truth had arrived. The gamble was about to pay off. Slocum glanced at the papers and saw three things: The shipping rate was $4.25, as Jackson said. The shipper was Earl Blake, destination Kansas City, consignee Ponca Enterprises. The last entry Slocum laid his green eyes on was the clincher. Five hundred head of Lean-to beeves were on their way to becoming steaks and ribs.

Lean-to!

He handed the papers to Fancher, who studied them without letting the rage he was feeling boil over. Fancher handed them back to Jackson with a courteous "Thank you."

Slocum turned to leave. "My apologies, Mr. Jackson. My partner and I will give the KP consideration—at four dollars and two bits a head, right?"

Jackson nodded. He was more pleased than he let on. The Atcheson, Topeka and Santa Fe was giving the KP stiff competition. The KP could make money at four twenty-five, so he had just corralled quite a bit of business for his firm.

He stuck out his hand, and Slocum tarried long enough to grasp it. He wondered, as he shook hands, whether Jackson knew the Blake–Ponca cattle were rustled. Probably not. That wasn't his concern. His concern was getting the beeves from here to there and making money for his bosses. Slocum briefly entertained the thought of letting Jackson know, but discarded the idea. Bringing up such a matter would only open a can of worms. He didn't want to make it any more complicated than it already was. Jackson would find out in time. Slocum would see to it.

As soon as they had cleared the place and were on their horses, Fancher let his anger explode.

"Damn Blake and Ponca," he swore. "They have the best of it all. They get the cattle free, and then a special rate to ship it. That alone probably makes them thousands of dollars. Damn it all to hell! Those bastards!"

"Agreed," said Slocum.

"Well, now that we have proof, let's get them."

"We don't have enough proof yet."

"I don't know what in hell could be more proof!" Fancher declared. "What do you want? Those names on that shipping list are plenty."

"It shows they shipped a lot of cows that were probably once yours. It shows that the two are in cahoots. We know it, but we couldn't convince a jury."

"Then what the devil are you going to do now?" Fancher was reverting to his excitable self.

"Go back to work in the yard."

"*What?* Now why in hell for?"

"If you don't stop acting like a kid, and get down off your high horse, I'm going to tape your mouth shut, boy!"

The two rode a little apart, both steaming. Then Fancher closed the gap. He was grinning.

"I sort of grow on you, don't I?"

Slocum stopped Wind, and faced Caleb.

"Listen," he said, "I have never seen anybody so likeable as you who can get on a man's nerves so much. Now I got a plan, but it calls for us to go back to the yards for a while."

"Can I ask why?"

"I want to watch for more Lean-to cattle. When they come, we'll act."

Fancher nodded. He glanced down over his fancy duds and sighed. "I knew they were too good to be true."

"You can leave the suit in the room and get it when all this is over."

They returned to the yard, and the Stetsoned boss had a fit. "You're late!" he bellowed.

"Yeah," said Slocum, "but we didn't go to California looking for gold."

"All right. Go check them cows they's loadin' now. Damn it all, anyway."

The cattle being loaded were from the Slash X outfit. According to Fancher, there were ten million of them.

"Oh, I'd say a few less, Fracas."

"Why did you give me a name like that?" Fancher was disgusted.

"Seemed appropriate, since you're always fracturing the peace."

The pens had been loaded again with bellowing cattle, and a new string started toward the chute. Slocum froze. These were Lean-to beeves. These were the animals he wanted to see. Here was proof on the hoof.

Fancher was excited. "Now what?" he asked. "How do we prove the brand has been changed?"

"If anybody's been changing brands around here, it's you, Fancher."

The man who had spoken charged at them like a wild longhorn. Slocum whirled to confront Paul Meers. Ten or fifteen men were with him, and none looked friendly, least of all Meers.

"It took me a long time," said Meers, "but by God I got you." He patted a coiled rope. "And for the party, I'm going to use this brand new neck catcher—your neck, by God."

As he spoke he drew his pistol, and so did the other men in his party.

"You outdrew Carp," he said. "Try it now, and you are both dead men."

16

Slocum felt the sweat ooze out of the pores of his skin, oiling his forehead, streaming over his scalp, soaking out of his chest. Only his palms were dry, and his finger itched to pull a trigger that would wipe the nightmare away.

Slocum had been in tight places before, but this was like a coffin, and the lid was about to be nailed down. There was no escape. A dozen guns covered him. He had fought his way clear countless times with fists or weapons or both. This time neither fist nor gun was going to do him any good. According to a rule of conduct he had formulated in the past, he reacted to circumstances, always keeping in mind, however, to take charge when possible. Violence was out so far as he was concerned in this circumstance. They only violence would come from the other side.

Whoever said it first, had a damned good point. Discretion sometimes *was* the better part of valor.

He glanced at Fancher. The young rancher seemed calm in the face of this life-threatening situation, but his hand was cupped above his gun butt. Slocum noted that the hand formed the typical Fancher claw. All of Caleb's practicing hadn't straightened those fingers out yet.

"Don't try it," Slocum told him. "We might get two or three, but I doubt it. Those lead balls travel at better'n nine hundred feet per second, I heard."

The claw relaxed, but Fancher's eyes burned, and his gaze never left Meers.

"No," Meers agreed, "don't try it." He nodded to a couple of men. "Get their guns."

Slocum gave his weapons to the men freely. Fancher followed suit. Slocum didn't like the feeling of being weaponless. He felt too light in the hips, almost naked, and a breeze blew through his nakedness. He stood exposed, but his mind was working. If power couldn't win, his wits would have to do the job.

"We aren't your men," he said to Meers. "You don't want us."

"That's a laugh," Meers snorted. He laughed to prove his point. His men joined in, and their laughter was mean —hanging mean. They wanted a "party," and they wanted it now.

"All you men lose cattle?" Slocum asked.

"All of us," snarled one. "Ever goddamned one of us has put silver in your pocket, Slocum, and now you're gonna pay—and pay big."

"Fancher here lost cattle, too. Why are you after him?"

"Because he's with you. You're two of a kind," said Meers.

"He lost ten thousand dollars. Do you think he'd stick with me if he thought I was a rustler?"

"It's a cover-up of some kind. He's in on it."

Meers's voice toughened. "Listen, two of the most respected men in the cattle business, Blake and Ponca, say you're guilty. I believe them. The marshal in Dodge says you're guilty. Four thousand in reward money for the pair of you says you're guilty, and my sixty-thousand-dollar herd, gone to God knows where, says you're guilty. What more proof do I need?"

"The marshal got his information from Blake and Ponca, right?" Slocum was forming a plan.

"Sure, who else? They were the ones who lost most."

"They never lost a thing," said Slocum. "But they made a few hundred thousand, believe me, and your beef helped bank that money, Meers."

"You're lying, Slocum." Meers nodded at the men with him. "Get 'em. We got a long trail back to Dodge." His eyes burned. "Most of us, that is."

"Wait!"

Slocum held up his hand in the cavalry signal to halt. He put authority and command into his voice. It was time to take charge.

"Meers," he said, "you come with me."

"Why in hell should I?"

"Aren't you going to give a practically dead man a chance, at least?"

Paul Meers thought it over. It was plain that he thought Slocum's request was a waste of time. Unexpected help came from one of his men.

"He's got a point, Meers," said the fellow. "I'd like to see the bastard hang, you bet." He had a long scar that divided his left cheek. He rubbed it. "But Blake ain't exactly lily-white, you know. I been hearing things about him."

"You hear things about all money men," snapped Paul Meers. "Ninety percent of it is envy talking."

"What about the other ten percent?" Slocum interjected swiftly.

Silence.

"All I'm asking is fifteen minutes of your time." Slocum pointed to the pens. "I want you all to see something first, and then, Meers, I want you alone for those fifteen minutes. If I can't convince you that Fancher, here, and me are innocent, *I'll* buy the rope."

"Good God, John," Caleb protested. "Let 'em use their own."

"All right," said Meers in a slow voice. "What do you want to show us?"

In the meantime, several men from the yard had gathered to witness the drama of a dozen men with drawn guns. The boss also arrived, his Stetson reflecting the yellow rays of a hot sun.

"What's going on here?" he demanded.

"These men want to look at those Lean-to cattle," explained Slocum.

"Can't have people running all over the place," protested Stetson. "Lots of valuable property hereabouts."

"We'll see them now, if you please," said Slocum, the polite words underlined by a commanding toughness. "Meers, you must have been deputized to head this posse. Use you pass."

Meers pulled his jacket aside to reveal a badge.

"These men," he said, pointing to Slocum and Fancher, "are rustlers. We're here to take them back to Dodge."

The boss of the yard swore, but in the face of the badge, there was little he could do.

"Look all you want," he agreed glumly. He cast a bitter glance at Slocum and Fancher. "And you were two of the best men I had. Jesus, you never know."

Slocum motioned Meers and his men to the pens.

"You see them?" he asked.

"Sure I see them—a bunch of cows. So?"

"Tell him, Fancher."

Caleb explained that the Lean-to brand was actually his Square U. His whole herd had been taken by outlaws, and the brand changed. He added that Meers and his men weren't the only ones looking for the guilty. He and Slocum had been searching, too, and the trail ended here, as far as his beef was concerned.

"Who is to say these aren't Lean-to cattle?" Meers demanded. "You're a suspected rustler yourself. Am I supposed to take your word against Blake's?"

"All right," said Slocum. "Now is when I need you for fifteen minutes alone."

"I don't know." Meers turned to his men. "What do you think?"

"Hell, man," said one, "what's fifteen minutes between a man and eternity?"

Meers grunted, what Slocum hoped was an affirmative sound.

"We'll just hold Fancher here," Meers said. "You know, as a kind of insurance. If anything happens to me, boys, you know what to do."

Fancher didn't exactly relish being "insurance," but he said to Slocum, "Good luck, my friend."

Slocum led the way back to the Kansas Pacific's office. Meers followed him upstairs to Jackson's office. Jackson was sitting at his oak desk in a cloud of Havana smoke. He glanced up, startled, when Slocum burst through the door.

"Here," he began, "you can't—"

Slocum cut him short. "Show this man those Lean-to shipping bills."

"Say, what's going on here? I showed them to you in confidence. I thought that confidence would be kept."

Slocum gave the KP man credit. Slocum had broken his word, and was getting a tongue-beating for it. Jackson might be a company man first and last, but he was not a coward.

Slocum admired guts, so he didn't like what he had to do next. He grabbed Jackson's shirtfront and pulled the man roughly out of his chair.

"Get those manifests," he said, "or I'll rip up this pretty shirt. Get them *pronto!*"

Jackson shook free, glanced at the grim-faced Paul Meers, and decided that perhaps this was not time for valor. He had done what he could. He found the papers and handed them to Slocum, who gave them to Meers.

Meers read them, then looked at Slocum, puzzled. "So

Blake ships Lean-to beef to Ponca. Somebody sells, somebody buys."

"The two of them are in on this rustling together," explained Slocum. "Blake does the dirty work, Ponca buys the beef."

"Hell, I need more proof than this. Maybe . . . maybe Blake bought these on the open market. Hell, I just don't know. I need solid proof."

"I figured you would, but I wanted you to see the paperwork first, so you'd get the connection."

Meers's voice took on an edge. "Either you get me more proof, or it's the end of the trail, Slocum."

"Come on."

"Where to?"

"We got to kill a cow."

They left Jackson smoothing his ruffled shirt and trying to figure it out by himself.

17

Lew Ponca took his ease in the lobby of the Dodge House. He smoked a cigar, just as Jackson of the KP did in Ellsworth, but the resemblance between the two men ended there. Jackson was as honest as possible and still rising on the Kansas Pacific ladder of success: Ponca wasn't bothered with a conscience, and wasn't too encumbered with emotions of any kind. He did like loose women and good whiskey, and substituted the physical pleasure they brought for emotion. The cigar he smoked was not a Havana. It was a darker, almost black leaf from far away Colombia. If it wasn't as sweet a smoke as a Havana, it proved much more valuable an asset. It was a conversation piece among the cattlemen with big money.

"Yuh say *Colombia?* Where in hell is that?"

Ponca would explain, and after his explanation there would be demands for some of the cigars. Ponca kept hundreds on hand. He would give out a few—grudgingly, it would seem to the recipient—and thus place the recipient in his debt. Ponca was well aware of the power of debt, even one so small as a few gift cigars. Men of honor paid their debts, and cattlemen, for the most part, were an honest lot. Without knowing they had been bought with a cigar, they would give Ponca business, deliver deals his way.

Ponca had the kind of mind that could turn a rank, black-leafed cigar into an asset.

The fact that his sister Vernine ran a bawdy house in Ellsworth didn't bother Ponca either. Uncharacteristically, he was fond of her, and wanted to see her safe in a dangerous business. He visited her as often as possible, and had been present when Slocum knocked at her door with the shotgun. Slocum hadn't seen him, but Ponca had seen Slocum through a side window. After returning to Dodge, Ponca had been the one to tell Meers where he could find Slocum, and probably Fancher, as well.

He took a long drag on his Colombian cigar, and the tobacco burned red hot. He blew the smoke into the air. Unlike Jackson's Havana, this smoke was not white, but yellowish in color. It had the power to stain walls, teeth, handkerchiefs, anything with which it came into contact. But Ponca didn't bother with the trivia of life. He was concerned with larger designs, such as making money, and seeing to it that his enemies were silenced. As a deputy, Paul Meers would have to return the criminals to Dodge for trial. Some of the men in his posse, however, were argumentative types. They might provoke differences of opinion, and have to fight Slocum and his sidekick. Fights often ended sadly for prisoners. Or perhaps the pair would try to escape. They could never outrun a .44 bullet.

Ponca would be surprised, indeed, to see Slocum and Fancher in Dodge again. There would most likely be an item in the paper telling how the two outlaws had escaped from Paul Meers's posse, but were hunted down and shot.

His thoughts returned to Vernine. If cigars were valuable, she was a gold mine. She ran a high-class bordello.

Only the wealthiest cattlemen knocked on her door and shared her wine. She was a capable girl with a good business head. She had been able to gather a group of prostitutes who looked as sweet and innocent as daisies in a field. This innocence sent many a rich buyer straight to Ponca. And many a wealthy seller, as well. Vernine got a percentage of the gross if any deals were consummated between the people she sent and Ponca or Blake. She was a great girl, and the brother and sister had been closer than anybody knew about, or would ever know about. Such matters, if made public, could ruin him in Dodge. As wild as the West professed to be—and it was plenty wild—such things were among the unthinkable. Only Blake suspected, but as soon as Blake's usefulness was over, he would become expendable. Ord Wade would earn his money, and the danger of Blake's using his suspicions in a blackmail scheme would be terminated.

Ponca had gotten rid of one Blake, Ned, when the man demanded more money. Blake had been mysteriously gunned down during the Pollywog affair, though he had had instructions to make himself scarce during the battle. Ned's death wasn't mysterious to Ponca, who had given the word to Wade to see to it. Wade had one of his boys provide Ned's exit. Even if the young Blake hadn't asked for a larger cut, he was doomed. Too many people were in on the deal, and too many tongues could wag at the wrong time, causing disaster. It was a matter of good business to eliminate some of the chance. The fewer who knew the better, and Ned had served his purpose. The Pollywog matter alone stood to net Ponca a hundred thousand in Kansas City.

Earl Blake, however, still had his uses. He knew the West, knew the cattlemen, knew how to rustle and how to cover up. Such experience was invaluable to Ponca, who knew only what he had learned in a year. And, somehow, he liked it better, being just outside the law. He gloated with the satisfaction of a man who thought he was above mortal considerations. Ponca felt that he was a cut above the ordinary man, more cunning, more resourceful, more powerful.

Blake, the fool, had fallen in love with Vernine. He'd left that sweet little filly, the schoolteacher, for a whore. It showed what kind of brains the man had. Vernine tolerated him because he was associated with the Ponca enterprises, but she ridiculed him behind his back. His short, thick neck was a source of lively laughter. And—this Ponca had from Vernine's own crimson lips—the man made love like a bull. *Hump—hump*, and it was over. Vernine would not miss Earl Blake.

Ponca smiled. All was right in his world. He crushed out his cigar in a tray and headed for his room. By God, this winter he'd be rich! Then he could get the hell out of this godforsaken land. He'd throw away the too-expensive boots that continually chafed his feet, and return to Washington, D.C. That was where things were moving. Talk of expanding the U. S. railroad system was becoming reality, and Ponca wanted a piece of that reality. He would take Vernine, and she could live with him as his housekeeper.

As Ponca got ready for bed, he smiled. Things were perfect. They would get much better.

Slocum cut a patch of hide off the longhorn he had just shot. He slid his knife deftly into the fat, separated it from the square chunk of cowhide. Then he scraped the underside delicately, revealing the brand, the true brand, underneath.

"I'll be damned," said Meers. The others in the posse crowded around and passed the damning proof from hand to hand. "Looks like we were wrong about this."

"Looks that way," said Slocum. "I reckon you can see the shape of the running iron those boys used. My herd will turn up the same way, I reckon."

"I'll buy you boys a drink," said Meers. "I want to hear what else you got to say. Boys, we made a mistake here.

How about if we put the hardware away and go to the saloon. My buy."

A chorus of shouts greeted this suggestion. Fancher smiled wanly. Slocum shot him a quick wink.

They talked through the afternoon, and Meers allowed as he had a couple of new friends. Fancher took a long time to get over his sulk. And he was still out his herd.

There came a time, that afternoon, to get down to brass tacks. Slocum leaned across the table in the Roundup Saloon and spoke his piece.

"You work with me," he told Meers bluntly, "and we'll get this whole mess cleared up in a couple of days."

"What are we supposed to do?" Meers wanted to know.

"Go to Hays and wait."

"Hays?"

"Hays."

"But why the hell there? That ain't noplace."

"It's closer to Dodge than Ellsworth is, right?"

"Yep."

"Then go to Hays and wait."

Meers remained uncertain. "What am I waiting for?"

"This train."

Meers scratched his head. "This train is going to Kansas City."

"No, it's going to Hays, and it's going to be carrying Lean-to—formerly Square U—stock on it. And then we are going to Dodge."

The light went on in Meers's eyes. "But how you going to get the train to Hays?"

"I'll find a way."

"We'll help," Meers said, indicating his men.

"No." Slocum smiled grimly. "This is something the law shouldn't know about."

The men shook hands. Meers paid the bill and the men poured out of the saloon and took up their horses at the hitch rail.

"I'll be seeing you, Meers," said John Slocum as he

settled into the saddle. Fancher wobbled a bit atop the outlaw horse, his face red from drink.

Meers sat his bronc, studying Slocum. He had never
met a man like John Slocum. Meers had wrangled his
spread out of the tough plains country year by year, acre by
acre. He had fought Indians, robbers, rustlers, trail bums,
and scamps for twenty years. He had fought the grangers
who tried to take his spread for farming, and fought the
Kansas legislature, which was gaining in granger power.
So far, he had held his own, lost a bit, won a bit, but the
battles had left him sure of only one thing: Paul Meers. He
knew Slocum was innocent. The man had shown proof
enough. But Slocum's plans were so wild that doubt, a
natural companion after all Meers had been through, took a
fighting stance.

"Damn," he growled, "I don't like it."

"Neither do I," agreed Slocum, "but I've got to do
something illegal to make the law see something illegal.
You know that." He glanced at the darkening sky. "Start
now, and I'll meet you in Hays by tomorrow night."

"By damn—you are going to nab a whole train?"

"If I have to."

Slocum waited, keeping his irritation concealed. He
wanted to grab the man as he had grabbed Jackson in his
office, and shake him. Every minute counted. If word
should get back to Dodge about the queer goings-on here
today, both Blake and Ponca would put it all together and
head for parts unknown. The death of Ken Dorsey and the
others would go unavenged. Fancher would never get his
herd back, or, if he did, it would take years of legal work
to do it. The same for Meers and all the cattlemen who'd
lost beef to Blake and Ponca. *Come on, Meers, I thought
we had a deal.*

The impasse was broken by one of the posse members.
"Hell," he said, "this is the shortest trail between two
points. I'm for it, Meers."

Several others agreed.

"We came a long ways for those two," said the posse man, "and they ain't the ones. Well, by God, *somebody* is, and my bet is they are in Dodge."

The grumbles snapped Meers out of indecision. He nodded.

"All right," he said, "it's crazy, but it's the only way. Let's hit it, boys."

"We got to eat first and get our horses fed, too," protested one man.

Meers glanced at Slocum, and from the glance, Slocum knew he was in charge, where he wanted to be.

"You can do that," he said. "Then ride like hell for Hays."

Slocum and Fancher stabled their horses. The freight train for Kansas City left at eight in the evening, and they wanted to be ready.

"I'll come back for you soon," Slocum told Wind. The horse munched oats and shifted his weight, nearly stepping on Slocum's foot.

"That's gratitude," said Slocum wryly. "Damn horse."

But he gave his animal a gentle pat as he and Fancher left.

"Now what?" Fancher asked.

"Haven't you been listening?" Slocum demanded, exasperated.

"Sure, but—"

"You can't believe we are going to steal a train?"

"That's it."

"Well, we are. What's more, it's carrying a lot of your beef on it."

"But . . ."

Slocum looked at the rancher. He had not, after all, asked if he would go along. He'd only assumed it.

"My friend," he said, "if you'd rather not, it's all right with me. We could end up dead or in jail. Stealing trains isn't everybody's job. I won't hold it against you if you'd rather not."

Fancher reddened.

"You're crazy," he shouted. "You know that? God damn it, you're crazy! But, like Meers says, it's the only way, so let's go."

"Good."

Slocum glanced at his watch. It was ten to eight. "It's time," he said, "for us to become engineers."

They reached the engine just as the engineer was cracking the throttle. The two climbed the metal ladder and stood in the cab with the engineer and the fireman.

"Here," said the engineer, a lanky man with a red kerchief tied around his neck, "what are you doing?"

Slocum pointed his Colt at the engineer.

"I'm sorry about this," he said, "but I am the new engineer."

The man gasped, and leaned back against the window. "Are you robbing us?" he gasped.

"No. We just want to borrow you."

"Borrow us?"

"Yes. Can you turn this thing around?"

"It would take some time."

"How long?"

"Maybe an hour."

"Forget it. We'll go to Hays backwards. Now put this smoke-eater in reverse, and let's get going."

The engineer glanced at his fireman. Staring into Fancher's .44, the fireman nodded.

Moments later, the train crew of Ellsworth was astonished to see the Kansas City freight speed backwards toward Hays. It was a sight, one of them explained afterwards, that made him wonder if he hadn't ought to give up visiting the Roundup Saloon forever.

18

The events Slocum had planned for the night went well. The train was not hindered in any way, General Colt commanding. As he traveled, Slocum had time to think. He thought about many things—Ken Dorsey, and Tubs and Bobby. He thought of them lying in a common grave, killed by people who considered killing a part of their game. They were senseless murders. Three young men cut down in their prime—in the cases of Bobby and Tubs, long before their prime. They were kids. Ken was older; he had tasted something of life. But even Ken was mostly untried, and life was all ahead yet. He had had big plans.

Slocum thought about Marisa with a mixture of sympathy and desire. She was alone now, and though Slocum was sure she could handle life on whatever terms it delivered, a little money in the bank wouldn't do her any harm. Money was a weapon of survival. Ken had left her some. Slocum might be able to help out, too.

Slocum saw the scattered lantern lights of the town and ordered the engineer to brake.

"We ain't in Hays yet," he said belligerently.

"You just brake us real slow and then hold up."

The backward train rolled to a slow stop, chuffing in heavy labor, shooting jets of steam into the predawn darkness.

Slocum left the engineer and the fireman with a warning. "If you step off this train, it'll go hard for you," he said. "We'll unload our beeves and you can head on back to Ellsworth."

"You'll never get away with this, mister," said the engineer.

"Thanks for the ride," said Slocum as he swung off the train and landed steady on his feet.

"Now what?" asked Fancher.

"We get those beeves unloaded pronto. Don't spook 'em, just open the gates and let 'em flood off. That engineer touches a valve, or the train moves, you come running back up here."

They unloaded the Lean-to beeves four miles from Hays. This was to lessen confusion, and to avoid the law which would be waiting. As they got the last of the cattle unloaded, Meers and his men rode up.

"You're going to have company pretty quick," said the rancher.

"The law?"

"They're a-comin'. Saw the train just after we did. I think somebody's been on the telegraph."

"Damn," said Fancher. "This ain't going to work, John."

"This is where you play your part," Slocum told Meers.

Meers met the marshal and two deputies.

"It's all right," he said.

"All right!" exploded the marshal, a sallow-faced man with a black handlebar moustache. "You people have sto-

len a train full of beef, for Christ's sake. What do you
mean, all right?"

Meers flashed his badge.

"I'm a deputy out of Dodge," he said. "These cattle
were rustled, and we are just taking them back."

"Why in hell didn't you go the regular route—down the
Chisholm and across?"

"Because we don't have time. This way is quicker."

"Sounds suspicious as hell to me," said the marshal.
"Why don't you just come with me, and we'll see about all
this?"

It wasn't an invitation. It was an order. Slocum tensed.
It meant more delay, and the longer the delay, the more of a
chance Blake and Ponca would get wind of the proceedings. Meers had done his part, but it wasn't enough. He
couldn't have the town marshal putting kinks in his rope.
He pulled his Navy Colt from its leather.

"We aren't going anywhere," he told the marshal. "But
you are."

"Where are we goin'?" demanded the lawman.

"To Dodge."

"Hey," said Meers, "I don't know about this. We can't
take a marshal and his deputies, Slocum. That's against the
rules, I believe."

"You have nothing to do with it," said Slocum. "I'm
taking responsibility."

He called to Fancher, who had dashed off on foot to
chase down a vagrant steer, more out of habit than anything else. "They all out?"

Fancher nodded. "I reckon."

"You give that engineer the high sign. Let him go."

"We brought you horses," said Meers. "That big bay
gelding over there rides good."

"Thanks," said Slocum.

He climbed into the saddle, glad to have something
under him. A moment later, Fancher climbed onto a pale

sorrel that was about fourteen hands high. The train groaned, its pistons chugged, and after a moment the wheels began to turn forward. The train moved slowly, then gathered speed, before it disappeared into the night. Slocum was damned glad the engineer hadn't blown his whistle. They might be there all night, rounding up cattle.

"Let's go," said Slocum.

Keeping his pistol on the three from Hays, Slocum ordered them to throw their weapons on the ground.

"You can pick them up when you get back," he said.

"You'll pay for this!" yelled the marshal. "My people will miss me, and come riding!"

"Not for a while," Slocum guessed. "I happen to know that officers of the law are gone a long time before they are missed. Not a whole lot of people care much, unfortunately."

The marshal snarled, ground his teeth, and reluctantly headed his horse south, following the beeves, which were already on the way.

"Damn you," he said. "You better be right in whatever it is you are doing."

"Yes," agreed Slocum, "I better be."

They arrived at Dodge the next morning after a hard twenty-four-hour drive. It was about ten o'clock, a time Slocum had deliberately picked. They drove the cattle down the main street and stopped in front of Dodge House.

Slocum could feel the tension mounting. He hoped to God that Blake and Ponca were present. He wanted them to be there to see the cattle they had stolen. They wouldn't have to be, but it would tie things up in a neat bundle. He and Fancher had discussed what they would do if Blake and Ponca were gone.

"I'd find them," said Fancher. "If they got word we were coming and they lit a shuck, I'd find them."

"Caleb, you wouldn't have a chance in hell against them—especially if Ord Wade was in their company. He's killed more men with his guns than he can count."

"Those people were responsible for stealing what was mine," said Fancher, with a hardness in his eyes to match Slocum's. "They need to pay for that."

"You talk pretty cocky," said Slocum. He was bone-tired and in no mood to humor the young rancher. Still, he admired the cattleman's eagerness. Fancher looked fresh, but he had come the same miles. Maybe he had the pepper to get him through this showdown.

"Just give me one shot," he told Slocum. "You said yourself that I was a good shot."

"Yes," said Slocum. "I told you that, and you are."

He also swore to himself that Fancher wouldn't be alone in his quest. He wanted those renegades as much as his young friend, perhaps more.

Blake and Ponca were there. So was Ord Wade, along with several other tough-looking individuals.

Hearing the racket, they gathered in front of the Dodge House to learn the cause. They were soon surrounded by a flood of cattle. One of Meers's men, riding in the vanguard, turned the leaders. The cattle began to mill, bawling and jostling one another, in front of the hotel. Slocum grinned, whispered something to one of Meers's men, then waved at the men gathered on the board porch.

"Get the marshal," yelled Blake on seeing Slocum. "There's our killer."

Meers spoke up. "I got him, Blake. Don't worry about it."

"Are these your cattle?" Slocum asked.

Blake stared at the brand. His head swiveled on his short neck, as his eyes traveled from cow to cow.

"Yes, those are mine. Lean-to cattle? I bought them a couple of weeks ago. What are you doing with them, Slocum?"

"Did you buy these from Blake?" Slocum directed his next question to Ponca.

"I buy all kinds of brands," said Ponca smoothly. "I might have bought them, yes."

"You *did* buy them, my friend. Shipping bills in Ells
worth show that."

"So what's this got to do with anything?" snappe
Ponca. He turned to Wade. "Go get the marshal."

"Stay right where you are," Slocum said gently. "I'r
not through with any of you yet. These," he said, pointin
at the cattle, "are Square U animals. They belong to m
friend here, Fancher. You, Blake, are the head of a rus
tling gang. You took my Pollywog, and changed it to Roll
ing Log. You killed three of my men, and Ponca had you
brother killed. I'd have no reason to kill my own man."

"You killed him; you wanted him," said Blake, uncer
tainly. "He knew what you were up to."

"Come on," said Slocum, "does that make sense? Yo
know I didn't steal those cattle, Blake. Think about it. Wh
would have had Ned killed, because he knew too much?"

Blake stared at Slocum for a moment. Then he turne
slowly to Ponca.

"The man's crazy," said Ponca. "Why would I want t
kill one of my own men?"

"Your man?" interrupted Slocum. "Now just whos
payroll was he on?"

"You can't prove those cattle are Square U," shoute
Ponca, beginning to lose some of his assurance.

"Wrong," said Slocum.

He walked his horse over to a whiteface, drew his pis
tol, and shot the cow dead. The noise startled the others
and they stampeded. Down the dusty street of Dodge the
raced, knocking over porch posts, trampling boardwalks
bawling, leaving great, steaming pies in the street.

"Go get 'em!" cried Meers. "We got 'em this far. W
don't want to lose 'em now."

Several men started after the panicked cows, but Slo
cum wasn't paying attention. He had an act of his own t
stage.

He dismounted and slipped his knife from its sheath
With quick dexterity, he slit a chunk from the hide of th

dead cow and skinned out the brand. He cut it off and held it up for Ponca and Blake to see. The underside of the hide showed the Square U plainly. They were old marks. The slanted roof that had turned the Square U into the Lean-to was red, to all eyes freshly made.

It was more dramatic the second time he did it. Fancher watched Slocum in awe.

"Do you see what has happened here?" Slocum asked the crowd at large. "This brand has been changed. These are Square U cattle."

There wasn't a man present who worked with cattle who didn't agree. For them, the evidence was as plain as a written confession.

Ponca, as green as he was, sensed that, and he turned to Blake, crying, "Why, you damned thief! I never had any idea!"

"You bastard!" raged Blake. "You're the brains behind this."

"No way to prove it," Ponca returned smugly. "I just bought the cattle, is all. I don't know where you got them."

"You also had Ned killed," said Blake, his short neck getting red. "You son of a bitch!"

"No proof I was involved in anything," Ponca insisted.

At that moment, a man came stomping quickly down the walk. He was carrying several running irons.

"I found these in Ponca's room," he hollered to Slocum, "just like you said. There was also one in Blake's room."

"Tsk, tsk," said Slocum triumphantly. "Now what would a couple of honest buyers be doing with such dishonest tools?"

Suddenly the atmosphere changed. Ponca stepped back behind Ord Wade and the hardcases flanking him.

"No you don't," cried Blake, "you're not getting away, Ponca. You sister lover!"

He started for his pistol.

"Don't!" cried Slocum.

Blake drew and pointed his weapon at Slocum. Before he could thumb the hammer, Slocum drew and fired. Blake's body shook from the impact of the .31. He stepped back once, and looked down at his chest, surprised. Blood was spreading over the front of his shirt.

"Why," he muttered, "I think I've been killed." Then he collapsed in the street.

For the next few seconds guns roared. Ord Wade drew and fired at Slocum, who felt the tug of lead at his shirt-sleeve. Fancher drew and fired at Wade. The two exchanged shots, and Wade stumbled backwards, crashing into a hitch rail. Slocum put another shot into him to make sure. Others were firing at him, too, but Meers had joined the fray. He and his men emptied the chambers of their six-shooters, and three more of Ponca's men writhed on the ground. This was too much for those still standing, and the gunmen fled.

"After them!" yelled Meers, and a dozen men dashed in pursuit.

Slocum eyed the bodies, noting the numbers with satisfaction.

"I guess that evens things up for my boys," he murmured. "Right, Caleb?"

There was no answer. Slocum turned quickly to see Fancher lying on his back.

"My God," said Slocum, "what the hell?"

He knelt beside his friend.

"Where'd you catch it?"

Fancher whispered his reply, "Where it counts, John. I got me the big one."

"Oh, come on," said Slocum savagely, "you're just nicked is all."

"Did I get Wade?"

"Yes, you got him. Now," he raised his voice, "let's get a doctor here. Quick. Quick, damn it!"

Fancher smiled faintly, and blood spilled from the corner of his mouth.

"At least," he said faintly, "I got one of them. I got one. You can have my ranch, John. Nobody there. You have . . ."

Caleb Fancher coughed, and a great spurt of crimson blood gushed from his mouth. He shuddered, then slowly relaxed in Slocum's arms.

He was gone. Slocum crouched over the young rancher's body, holding him close. In his heart there burned a great hate for all people like Blake, Ponca, and Wade.

"Jesus," he said, "sweet Jesus."

He knew it wasn't over yet. Not by a long shot.

19

Slocum let Fancher's body down gently. He rose and stared at the scene around him. People were beginning to crowd in, and the marshal from Hays was screaming, "Arrest that man!" and pointing at Slocum.

The Dodge marshal arrived on the run and headed for Slocum immediately. Slocum was in no mood for this, and he lifted the flap over the butt of his other Colt. Meers saw the action and intervened.

"Things aren't what they seem, Jim," he said to the Dodge lawman. "Slocum's innocent. So was Fancher."

"I can take your word for it, Meers?" It was plain that the marshal didn't like it any.

"You can."

"Who started this fight?"

"Blake drew first," said Meers. "There are a dozen witnesses."

The marshal nodded, and walked among the bodies.

"Blake and Ord?" he asked, viewing the corpses.

173

"And Ponca," said Meers.

Ponca!

In his concern over the death of Fancher, Slocum hadn't thought of Ponca.

"I don't see him here," said the lawman. "He must have got away."

Slocum stalked among the bodies, looking and looking again, for some had half their faces blown away. There was no doubt about it. Ponca was not among the dead.

"Well, I'll be damned," he swore softly.

The man who had been ultimately responsible for the whole thing had escaped. The rattlesnake had found its hole, the scorpion its nest, after delivering the poison and death to the world.

"You better get that fixed," Meers said, indicating Slocum's wound.

It wasn't serious, but it needed the attention of a doctor to stop the bleeding. Slocum had only one shirt, the one he wore, and he didn't want it all stiff with blood. He thought about that. No, he had two shirts. The other was in the Ellsworth hotel room, along with his and Fancher's new suits. Poor Caleb would never wear that suit again. He had sure been proud of those new duds. It was then that Slocum decided Fancher would have his suit. He'd see to that.

But not now. Fancher would have to be buried. The doctor and the undertaker were already there, moving among the dead men, feeling pulses that weren't there, examining fatal wounds.

Slocum spoke to the undertaker about Caleb.

"You take him first," he said, "and I want a burial today."

"Impossible," said the undertaker.

"Anything is possible," Slocum told him, and his green eyes hardened. "I want a grave for him, a cross, and the ceremony, all within the next two hours."

"Impossible," the undertaker repeated.

Slocum stepped close to the man, chest to chest, and

bored into the other's eyes with his own. Slocum's rage smoldered in the green depths. His grief burned and his hate was exploding. There was death in those eyes, or, at the least, a broken arm, and the undertaker got the message.

"All right," he said hastily, "I'll do what I can."

"I don't expect these special services for nothing," Slocum told him. "Here." He handed the man some gold coins. "This should cover it."

The undertaker smiled after glancing at the yellow metal, and Slocum wanted to hit him. The son of a bitch was happy to get that death money. God damn him and his kind! But he didn't hit him. Instead, he said, "You be at the cemetery in two hours."

"Yes, sir."

Slocum waited until the doctor had examined the bodies. He stood a little aside, not wanting to move among the depressing silence of people who were no longer people. He did take one more look at Blake and Ord. They seemed peaceful. It was as if they slept, as if they were children. Slocum had noted before how much like children's faces the faces of dead adults were. Maybe somewhere they were starting over as children. Perhaps this time they would keep their innocence, but Slocum doubted it. This was a hard world, and innocence had to fight hard to keep its identity. Fancher had been as close to an innocent man as Slocum had seen in a long time. The young rancher wasn't an angel, but there was a naïvete about him that was as close to innocence as the world he lived in would allow.

Or maybe he was a real angel now. Slocum shrugged off his thoughts. He was giddy and lightheaded from the hard ride, from the loss of blood. He blinked to clear his head. The sound of gunshots still rang in his ears and he couldn't shake it out. His nostrils still burned with the acrid taint of burnt black powder, and his eyes stung with the white smoke that had filled the street for a few terrible seconds.

After the doctor had finished with the dead, he took Slocum to his office and mended the torn skin.

"An inch over," the doctor told him, "and your arm would have been shattered. Maybe lost the use of it. You were lucky."

Slocum agreed. He had been damned lucky. He paid the doctor, then bought a new shirt and went to see Marisa.

"I heard the shooting," she told him after a loving kiss, "but I didn't want to go and see who it was. I thought it might be you."

"I was there, yes."

"Blake and Ponca?"

"Blake will be buried in a day or two, I guess. Ponca got away."

"The one who shouldn't have!"

"I'll get him. I know where he is."

Marisa kissed him again, and Slocum felt desire flooding his veins.

"Come," she said softly, "you're tense and tired, and also sad. Come."

They made love quickly, not because Slocum wanted it that way, but because he had things to do, and not much time left. There was Fancher's funeral to attend, and he was going to Ellsworth immediately afterwards. Ellsworth held the final chapter in the book.

At the door, he kissed Marisa goodbye.

"Will I see you again?" she asked.

"I don't know, but Ken had a percentage of the drive, so you'll have money coming when this is all cleared up. If I don't bring it, it will be deposited to your account at the bank."

"He never told me about a percentage."

"Ken never talked much."

That wasn't the truth, since Ken Dorsey liked nothing better than to talk about his plans.

Marisa smiled. She pressed her lips against Slocum's again.

"How I wish you'd stay," she murmured. "We could have a good life together."

"I know," Slocum replied quietly, "but for a man like myself . . . Well, perhaps I'm not quite ready. Can you understand that?"

"No, but I'll have to live with it, won't I?"

The girl squeezed his hand, and Slocum left. He knew he was leaving a special woman. He knew he might never meet another woman like Marisa Dorsey. But he had things to do, deadly things, and closer involvement with Marisa might bring her only more grief. There was enough grief in her life now, with the loss of Ken and his dreams. No need for more.

It was nearly time for Fancher's burial, so Slocum went directly to the cemetery. The undertaker was present, and a grave had been dug. Meers and several of his men stood by silently, out of respect, perhaps. Fancher's body lay in a wooden casket. The lid had been nailed down.

"Open it," ordered Slocum.

"But . . ." the undertaker began, then changed his mind when Slocum's green eyes flashed. He nodded to one of the gravediggers, who pried the lid loose with the point of his shovel. Fancher lay there, his young face peaceful.

"Goodbye, my friend," Slocum said quietly, then turned to the undertaker. "All right. Put the lid back on, and get on with it."

The ceremony was brief. The undertaker serving as parson, read a few words from the Bible. Slocum scarcely heard them. It didn't matter. If there was a God, Caleb Fancher would be allowed in His company, Slocum reckoned, because Fancher had been a good man.

"Do you want to say a few words over your friend before he returns to the earth from whence he came?" asked the undertaker, his voice sepulchral.

Slocum was surprised. He fumbled with the brim of his hat and shuffled his feet.

"Yeah, I reckon," he said, his voice thick. He looked

around at the men gathered there, then at the coffin.

"Caleb Fancher was one hell of a man," he said gruffly, choking back tears. "He ran good cattle on his spread, cattle that was stolen from him. He learned how to use a gun and he had blood in his eye when he was shot down in cold blood. He was fast and he proved that, Lord. Give him a good place in your heaven and pick a special place in hell for the bastards who put out his lamp before he had a chance to live out his life. He's a man to ride the river with and I want him treated special."

Slocum choked and turned away, red-faced, fighting his emotions. He looked at the men gathered there. There wasn't a one of them who didn't have his eyes brimful of tears. None of them looked away, but Meers snuffled and wiped his eyes with his sleeves.

"I reckon that's it, then," said Slocum. "Much obliged you all came to say a last goodbye to my friend."

When Slocum looked up at the sky he knew he had never seen it so blue. It was blue as cornflowers, and he felt the breeze blow over the graveyard and tug at his sleeve like an unseen hand. He put his hat back on, squared it, and stalked from the graveyard toward the horse Meers had given him.

"I'll see you in town, Slocum," said Meers awkwardly.

Slocum nodded, but rode off onto the prairie, away from town, where the wind was stiffer and he could be alone with his thoughts.

When he returned to town, Meers was waiting for him at the Drover's Saloon. Slocum hitched his horse next to the rancher's.

"I got the marshal here to look into the accounts of Ponca and Blake," said Meers. "When it's all unraveled, we'll get some of our money back." He hesitated. "I don't know what to do about Fancher's."

"Keep it here in the bank," said Slocum. "He gave me his ranch. You heard his last words."

Meers nodded.

"I'll go down there after I leave Ellsworth and see who is to get what."

Meers nodded again, but added, "You sure Ponca has gone to Ellsworth?"

"Yes. It's the only place he can go right now. He'll get his money and clear out. He'll try to head east for cover, if I reckon right."

"That was a foolish thing to do, maybe."

"What's that?"

"Go to that boy's funeral. Ponca's got a good head start on you."

"Some things a man's got to do in turn. Caleb would have done the same for me."

"You didn't know him for very long." It was a flat statement, but Slocum could tell that Meers was curious. He was, himself. He had thought about it a lot out there on the prairie, after the funeral.

"Hell," Slocum laughed, "you get to know a man pretty well if you've been through what me and Fancher suffered."

"Chasing after the rustled cattle?"

"No." Slocum grinned. "Spending three weeks in a damned line shack eating beans and jackrabbits."

Meers smiled and nodded. "I know what you mean, John." It was the first time he had called Slocum by his given name.

Meers stuck out his hand, and Slocum took it.

"You take care of the money end of this?" Slocum asked.

"Yep. I owe you that. Take that horse, too. It's yours."

"I was going to pay you for it."

"No, he's yours. Ride careful, John Slocum."

Slocum nodded and went his way. He bought provisions, filled his canteens, and grained his horse. He had forgotten to ask Meers if the animal had a name. No matter. He would give it one, or sell it when this was all over. He might even call it Caleb.

He saddled up and rode out of Dodge without looking back. There were those who looked at him as he passed with new respect, but it was their town, not his. It was their town and it had claimed his friend's life, had Slocum's own blood on its dusty street. He pointed the horse toward Ellsworth.

His thoughts turned to Lew Ponca. The man was entirely capable of bushwhacking him on the trail, or even from some hidden corner in Sally's. If so, then that was how it would be.

Slocum didn't think about it too much. That was wrong thinking, and wrong thinking made cowards of men.

20

Slocum began calling the big bay gelding Caleb. He wondered if he wasn't a little addled, but just saying the name made him think of his friend, kept Fancher close and alive in his heart. The horse didn't have the stamina of Wind, but he rode well as long as he was rested, watered, and grained.

He rode at night and in the cool of the day, and rested in the heat, when the horse grew tired. He let the sun and the wind heal his slight arm wound, felt the pain gradually go away and the flesh close up and scab over. He didn't push the horse or himself, because he had a hunch that Ponca thought he was dead, since he didn't pursue him immediately. Still, they made it to Ellsworth in three days. On the way, Slocum passed the camp where Ponca and Blake had kept their rustled merchandise. There wasn't a cow in sight, nor a bedroll or a campfire. A few scattered artifacts told of human occupation—a sock with too many holes in it, a few empty .44 casings, remains of branding-iron fires.

Except for these, there was only the Kansas flatlands, and the ever-present wind. It made a mournful sound, a grave-yard sound, eerie, and Slocum hurried on through. There was nothing to be gained in lingering except bitter and sad memories.

He arrived in Ellsworth at night, and lodged his horse at the livery. He wanted to arrive at Sally's on foot; no sense in making an easy target of himself atop the bay, and by now everyone knew his spotted horse. Wind was in the same stable. On sensing Slocum's presence, he whickered. Slocum gave him a pat and said, "I'll be back soon, boy, and we'll get the hell out of here."

He walked over to Sally's and entered without knock-ing. Vernine was talking to a customer. By the dress of the man, Slocum guessed he was a wealthy rancher or buyer. Several other women sat around the room in various poses. They smiled at Slocum, but Vernine was startled.

"Slocum!" she exclaimed. "I thought you were . . ."

"Dead?" Slocum finished for her.

"I heard about the fight," she said, "and that you were hit."

"I was, but not that bad. Your brother has been doing some wishful thinking."

Vernine flushed. "You'll have to take one of the other girls. I'm busy."

"I want you, and you know it."

The customer spoke up. "Now, see here! I've been making sweet talk with this little lady, and she has agreed to accept my company for the evening."

"Shove your sweet talk up your ass," said Slocum pleas-antly. "This 'little lady,' as you call her, is coming with me."

The other man's face turned red, and he started to huff and chuff. It looked like a full-blown argument until Ver-nine stopped it. "Look, Bill," she said to the customer, "I really do have to see this man. Why don't you take Lillie and Dorine over there?" She pointed to two of the prettiest girls. "You can have them both for the same fee."

"Two?" The man's interest suddenly swept away from Slocum to the girls. "Two?" he repeated.

"Two," said Vernine sweetly, "and they'll give you a good time, Bill. They know just how to please you."

The man nodded, but as he joined the two girls, he blustered to Slocum, "Good thing Vernine knows how to handle things like this, or you wouldn't be anything but wolf-meat hash for my cowhands, fellow."

Slocum ignored him, and steered Vernine to a back room.

As soon as they were alone, he asked, "Where is he?"

"Where's who?"

Vernine put her arms around Slocum's neck and drew him down. She kissed his lips. The scent of her almost suffocated Slocum, but he pushed her away.

"You know who," he said. "Your brother, Lew. He's here, and I know it. Unless you've already sent word that I'm in town, and he's run out."

"He's not here," Vernine insisted.

She slipped out of her dress and hung it over the back of a chair.

"You could have signalled one of your girls to warn him. And you must know I'm not going to waste time in talk when I see him."

Vernine poured two glasses of wine, and handed one to Slocum. He accepted it.

"Let's not speak of unpleasant things," said Vernine. "Let's drink to this meeting." She caressed his neck, and Slocum had to fight down the desire that rose up in his veins like summer heat.

"Drink," whispered the girl, and she sipped her wine.

Slocum tasted his.

Vernine kissed him again.

"God," she whispered, "you make me hot."

She set her glass on a bureau, and undressed as Slocum watched. He felt his passion rise, when the girl stood

naked in front of him. She had large, pendulous breasts
and the nipples stood erect and pert. Her stomach was flat
like the stomach of a woman in her twenties, which Slocum was sure she was not, and the dark triangle of hair
rising from the valley of her thighs was moist.

"I've never been so hot," she murmured huskily, lying
on the room's main piece of furniture, a bed. "Come."

She extended her hand to Slocum and spread her legs
for him. For a moment, just for a moment, Slocum weak-
ened. He wanted Vernine Ponca, and for a moment he
nearly forgot his mission.

But he hesitated, and hesitation, he had learned long
before, was a stumbling block to the culmination of passion. Thoughts crowded in to push aside the main drive of
the moment. Ken Dorsey's dead face came to mind, and
those of Tubs, Bobby, and Caleb Fancher.

Slocum's passion eased back to a controllable level, and
he said coldly, "I didn't come here to make love to you. I
came to kill your brother."

Vernine's stare turned to a glare of hot hatred. With a
scream, she snatched a revolver from under her pillow.
Slocum knocked it from her hand, and she bit him.

"You bitch," he growled, and slapped her.

She fell back to the sound of a new voice.

"Vernine—not with *him!* For God's sake, not with
him!"

Slocum whirled to face Lew Ponca. The man was staring at the naked body of his sister.

"You'd make love to him?" he asked in complete disbe-
lief. "You'd go to bed with the man who is here to kill
me?"

"I was just getting him on our side," said Vernine. "This
is the only way I know how."

"Almost worked," said Slocum, keeping a wary eye on
Ponca.

The man stood in the doorway, anger and hurt showing
plainly in his handsome face.

"My God, Sis," he said, "after all we've been to each other, you'd do it with him?"

Suddenly, he drew his pistol, but Slocum was on him in seconds, his powerful arms pumping fists as hard as pine knots. Ponca dropped, and Slocum quickly scooped up the pistol. He drew his own.

"Now," he said, "how in hell am I going to kill you, Ponca? You're unarmed."

"But she isn't," said Ponca.

Slocum turned to Vernine, and realized his mistake as soon as he did so. From the corner of his eye, he saw Ponca draw a derringer. The next moments were burned in his mind forever after.

He dove across the bed just as Ponca fired his deadly little weapon. The bullet missed and struck Vernine in the chest. Slocum fired across his body at Ponca. Ponca's derringer bucked a second time, and Slocum felt a jar in his arm—the one that had already been tagged by Wade's bullet. He thumbed the hammer back on his Colt for a second shot, but it wasn't necessary. Lew Ponca had crumpled to the floor, and Slocum knew by the stillness of the body that the man would never voluntarily move again.

He turned to Vernine, lying still and quiet on the bed, blood soaking her breasts and the linen.

He took her up in his good arm. "Vernine?"

She opened her eyes. "Is he dead?"

Slocum nodded.

At that moment Merry Lynn Adams burst through the door. She carried a shotgun, and her face was a mask of hatred. She stumbled over Ponca's body, and the shotgun discharged, tearing great holes in the ceiling.

She stared at the bloody scene before her, and sucked in a hard breath.

"My God," she whispered, and glanced down at Ponca. "Is he dead?"

"He's dead," said Slocum. "You came for your revenge?"

Merry nodded.

"You," said Slocum, "are a little late. Vernine is badly hit."

Merry nodded again, but she leaned against the door for support. "I never realized it would be so . . . so . . ."

"Bloody?"

Merry nodded. "Yes," she said faintly.

"Gunshots do that," said Slocum. "Revenge is not so sweet, girl."

Vernine stirred. "Lew?"

"He's dead," Slocum informed her a second time, his voice gentle.

The girl smiled weakly. "Then I'm glad I'm going, too."

She tried for air, one last breath, but it wasn't there, and she slumped over, never to rise again.

"Well," Slocum whispered, "maybe it was best."

His arm was leaking a lot of blood, and he felt dizzy. Still, he was aware enough to know that the law had arrived. The law had been looking for Lew Ponca, and it seemed it was all right that things had turned out as they did.

"Save the people a lot of tax money in trials and all that," grumbled a male voice. "We got the whole story over the telegraph from Dodge."

"You didn't come to arrest me?" asked Slocum, incredulous.

"No, we know what you did. We got a good town here, but we can't keep all the rats out. We find 'em, we get rid of 'em."

"Well, I'll be damned," said Slocum softly.

Maybe he had been wrong about these Kansas cowtowns. After all, it wasn't their fault that men like Ponca and Blake sullied them up. Ellsworth was cleaning up the picture it presented to the world. Whorehouses, even high-class ones like Vernine's, were on the way out. The vice that had once brought good coin to the town was giving way to a more orderly way of making money: farming. Farming was next to cattle in income, and cowboys were numbering their days. Long drives were nearing a time of decline as railroads spread throughout the Southwest.

Slocum strode through the gathering crowd of gawkers, walked through the empty parlor, so tawdry and quiet now. He opened the door and heard footsteps behind him.

"Where are you going?" asked a breathless Merry.

"Thought I'd look up a sawbones, get him to stitch me up before I leak all over town."

"Wait, I'll go with you," she said, and took his arm. Slocum fought off the dizziness, tried not to lean on her.

The doctor took six stitches to close the wound. Merry sat with him as he drank the whiskey and gritted his teeth.

As they were leaving the doctor's office, the girl paused. Her face was pale, but she had regained her composure. "I guess Earl is dead, too?" she asked.

Slocum nodded.

"I won't ask who killed him," Merry said.

"No. It's over now, and nothing can change what has happened."

She clung to his good arm when they stepped out into the cool night air.

"We'll go to my place," she said. "You need lots of rest."

"Will I get it?"

"That's up to you."

A moment later she added, "It was horrible."

"Think of what your shotgun would have done, Merry."

The girl shuddered. "I'm so glad I never did it. So glad."

"I told you that revenge can backfire, like the tip of a bullwhip."

"Yes."

As they walked toward Merry's place, Slocum heard a steer bawl in the loading pens. A dog barked, and a voice spoke once, then cut itself short. Excited people were

moving toward Sally's, and an engine blew its whistle, a
lowing sound, the sound of cattle in pain.

To Slocum, it was the loneliest sound in the world. It
spoke of the past and the present, but it spoke most of all to
the future. The future, in that mournful wail, came across
to Slocum as haunted, and he felt like he was alone in the
graveyard of the world.

The next day, he picked up Fancher's new clothing at
the hotel. Then he and Wind left town. When he was several miles out, Slocum burned the suit and all the garments
that had once graced the frame of Caleb Fancher.

As the cloth turned to ash, the smoke danced in the
wind and spread across the sky like a shroud. The shroud
widened and spread a thin gauze across the sun, turning the
sun pale yellow.

Slocum spoke.

"I told you that you'd get your suit again, Caleb. Wear it
well, my friend."

He stood for a while, until the ashes of the fire grew
cold. Then he headed south to the Square U, under a sky so
blue it hurt to look at it. It hurt him to think that he would
see the ranch for the first time without Caleb Fancher,
without hearing his voice. He would remain there for a
while, but his days there would be numbered and sad, for
Slocum knew that the restlessness which governed his life
would return.

He would move on.